NANCY HARTRY

SMOKESCREEN

Tundra Books

Published in Canada by Tundra Books,
a division of Random House of Canada Limited,
One Toronto Street, Suite 300, Toronto, Ontario M5C 2V6

Published in the United States by Tundra Books of Northern New York,
P.O. Box 1030, Plattsburgh, New York 12901

Library of Congress Control Number: 2012949903

Library and Archives Canada Cataloguing in Publication

Hartry, Nancy
Smokescreen / by Nancy Hartry.

ISBN 978-1-77049-405-3. – ISBN 978-1-77049-406-0 (EPUB)

I. Title.

PS8565.A673S56 2013   jC813'.54   C2012-906502-1

We acknowledge the financial support of the Government of Canada through
the Canada Book Fund and that of the Government of Ontario through the
Ontario Media Development Corporation's Ontario Book Initiative.
We further acknowledge the support of the Canada Council for the Arts
and the Ontario Arts Council for our publishing program.

ONTARIO ARTS COUNCIL
CONSEIL DES ARTS DE L'ONTARIO

**This novel is entirely a work of fiction. Ontario has no
Department of Forestry and Parks. Any resemblance to persons
living or dead is purely coincidental.**

Cover designed by Terri Nimmo
Text designed by Rachel Cooper

www.tundrabooks.com

Printed and bound in the United States of America

1 2 3 4 5 6   18 17 16 15 14 13

For Kathy,
who knows that anything can happen

ACKNOWLEDGMENTS

Many generations of black bear were born during the time it took to make this book. And many trees were pulped. There are so many people to thank.

First and foremost to "the goup" — Susan Adach, Ann Goldring, Loris Lesynski, Teresa Toten. Thank you for hanging in through many renditions and cheering me on.

Thanks to my readers: Maxine Hartry, Doug Hartry, Lesley Marshall, Susan Foley and Carol-Faye Petricko. Particular thanks to Beth Pollack and Louise Pyne for their insightful criticisms and encouragement when I needed them most. Jocelyn Burke — you are a talented editor and thank you for your voice and your inspiration. Many thanks to Denis Durocher for making sure my French is correct, for your editorial suggestions, and your input into the cover.

To Jennifer and David Coulter who opened their home to me at least twice, giving me a quiet and nurturing place to work.

Thanks to Yvonne Thompson for being my 'cloud' before that was a concept.

Many thanks to my technical experts — to T.M. for his fire fighting expertise; to Brian Jones, bush pilot and retired Air Canada pilot for solving my plot problems. It would have been a very different book without your help. Finally, to Kathy Thom — between the two of us, we managed to come up with one coherent memory.

To my teachers — Peter Carver, Kathy Stinson, Paula Wing, Barbara Greenwood and Sarah Ellis, and all their students who helped workshop this book. It took a city.

For their editorial support — Kathryn Cole, Sue Tate, Tara Walker, Samantha Swenson and in particular Gena Gorrell for bear wrestling *Smokescreen* into shape.

Finally, to my children, Gaelan Burke and Jocelyn Burke, and my husband, Frank Burke for enduring my inattention and glazed looks while I hitched a ride with Kerry and Yvette as they bombed the lakes and rivers of northern Ontario. One day, I hope to share them with you.

PROLOGUE

A hot wind blew and there was a whispering across the island and the lake. The round leaves of the poplar trees twisted, making soft clapping sounds, as if the bush knew.

Clap. Clap. Clap.

Something must be coming.

Something must be coming.

Two loons, wings a blur, skimmed the water, fleeing because they could.

The first lick of fire was a tendril of smoke from under a mat of birch leaves and pine needles. *Poof!*

The flame spread along the ground, an orange flare as small as the flick of a cigarette lighter. In seconds there was another and another, until a jack pine, its resin oozing in the heat, sparked like a Roman candle. Flames licked up the bark, along the lowest limbs, to be handed off to the outstretched arms of the pine's nearest neighbor.

Up, up, up the fire climbed to the crown and skipped from tree to tree.

There was a roar as the oxygen was sucked out of the forest. The crackling of debris and the thud of branches plummeting to the forest floor masked the frantic cries from the birds and animals. The whisperings of the fire, the popping of seed pods, told every living creature to run for its life.

One tendril of smoke. One flame from a Bic lighter. And *clap, clap, clap* . . . there she goes.

PART 1

The Bunkhouse

June 27–28

CHAPTER 1

A line of blood leaked from a puncture just below Kerry's knee. She hadn't felt the bug bite until the dribble of blood tickled her skin. When she swatted her leg at yet another fly, her palm was smeared red. Kerry spit on a tissue and began erasing the bloody smudge where a tiny blackfly had neatly taken a chunk out of her, leaving her leg itchy and throbbing.

Kerry had been sitting on the bunkhouse steps for three hours, ever since her exasperated supervisor had dumped her there to wait for her "partner in crime," as he put it. Her prospective partner for the summer hadn't shown up for work yet, and the boss said he was damned if he was going to do the orientation twice. "Over my dead body, no matter what those idiots in charge of the Student Employment Program have to say about it," he grumbled, and drove off to his office in town.

Frustrated, Kerry kicked the duffel bag she'd so carefully packed just yesterday in Toronto. She'd taken a checklist of camping essentials off the Internet and followed it exactly, but the bug spray that was so highly recommended seemed useless against the bloodthirsty blackflies of Northwestern Ontario.

More than once, she'd slipped the straps of her pack over her shoulders and made to leave for home. All she had to do was walk down that gravel lane hemmed in by evergreen trees to the Trans-Canada Highway, turn right, and go directly to the Greyhound bus depot in town. Do not collect five thousand dollars for a summer job as a cottage development technician with the Department of Forestry and Parks, whatever that meant.

But Kerry wouldn't give her mother the satisfaction of seeing her fail. It was unbelievable how her mother had schemed and pulled strings to get Kerry this job. "Well, you could have pulled harder and found me something better!" Kerry said, and then covered her mouth and looked to see if anybody had heard her. There were only the bugs and the birds and the trees, of course. So many types of evergreens.

The living compound for student employees was almost surrounded by bush. A long gravel laneway extended north from the highway through the woods and ended in a circular parking lot bordered by white clapboard buildings. On the north were a construction trailer and a separate cabin that housed a washroom. On the east was the cookhouse, complete with screen door and windows outlined in forest green paint, and on the west, where Kerry had been told to stay put, was the "boys bunkhouse." It was reserved for fire crew, parks staff, and conservation officers.

"It'll be just you two girls over on that side," Buzz Harcourt, the supervisor, had said. "We thought we'd put you up in the construction trailer because it's close to the washroom. We were told to build a *separate* washroom just for you, and I don't mind saying it blew my budget. I hope you like it."

Kerry knew what he was really saying was "You'd better appreciate it," but she didn't know how to respond so she said nothing at all.

She'd visited the washroom three times in the past hour and there was nothing special about it. There were two sinks and two toilet cubicles partitioned by plywood that had been hastily primed, the floor was of sheet vinyl, and the lighting consisted of two bare lightbulbs hanging from the ceiling. She'd checked three times but found no lock on any of the doors, not the outside door, nor the cubicle doors. The metal shower stall tucked in a corner had a clear plastic shower curtain, but there was no covering at all on the window.

Kerry blew her bangs off her forehead, trying to calm herself. How was she going to survive in this nowhere camp? And what did she know about being a cottage development technician? Nothing! As she sat down on the ground and put her head between her knees, slowing her breathing to avoid a full-blown panic attack, her brain seized on one little detail the boss had mentioned about her partner: she'd grown up in a construction camp in Labrador. *Thank you. She has experience. She'll show me how.* "Come on, you can do it!" she said out loud. She found herself saying this daily, since bombing out the month before in the biggest Irish Dance competition of her life. It should have been the pinnacle of fourteen years of practice. Instead it had ended in an embarrassing fall, and she'd been carried off the stage. *My body betrayed me. Correction, my mother overtrained me. And now I have shin splints! Stress fractures, according to the doctor. Nice move, Mother, packing me off to this place in the middle of nowhere, so I'm out of your sight. If I can't dance, I'm nothing to you.*

For the twentieth time, Kerry tried texting her dance friends and got a "no service" response. *Long distance is probably a fortune from here,* she thought, but tried calling anyway. No luck. *Maybe if I change locations.* She walked down the strip of grass between two gravel ruts leading from the camp to the highway. Out of nowhere, a cloud of blackflies swarmed her head, invading her ears and lungs. She broke into a run to elude them, and when she reached the highway she bent double and flipped her long hair over her forehead, scrubbing her scalp with her nails to drive the bugs away.

As she stood up again, Kerry was startled by the air brakes of a Greyhound bus stopping not far from her. The door opened and an enormous backpack and fluorescent green day pack flew out onto the shoulder. A girl wearing four-inch black wedges and carrying a Holt Renfrew shopping bag came down the steps. Kerry saw her laughing, probably at something the bus driver was saying. The girl turned and pouted, then blew a kiss in the direction of the open door. Only when the door closed and the bus pulled away did she deal with the equipment at her feet.

Damn, just a hitchhiker, and not my missing partner. What kind of idiot wears heels like that in the bush? Kerry turned toward the compound, steeling herself for the run back through the woods.

"Yoo-hoo, I can take some help here, please. Hello, hello! You think I'm talking to the trees?"

The girl looked as if she'd walked straight off the cover of *Vogue* magazine. Her v-necked salmon pink shirt was silk, and it matched shorts barely covering her butt. Her fingers and toes were painted the same color, all except the big toe on each foot, which was a bright, metallic blue. Kerry couldn't see the girl's eyes because they were concealed behind wraparound Gucci sunglasses, but she sensed that she was being checked out in turn.

"You like that color on my toes, eh? Me, I think it works."

"It's nice," said Kerry. "You shouldn't have any trouble getting a ride into town. It's only about a mile and a half, and there's lots of traffic along this part of the Trans-Canada."

"But I'm already here. This is the Department of Forestry and Parks, *non?*"

"Not really, the office is in town. This is just a camp."

"Perfect. I'm here to find cottage sites."

Kerry looked blank.

"I'm the cottage development tech."

"No way," said Kerry. "You can't be. The supervisor said there are only two, and . . ."

"And I'm one of them. Yvette Bernier. You?"

Embarrassed, Kerry barely took the outstretched hand. "Kerry Williams from Toronto. How come you're so late?"

Yvette shrugged. "I couldn't help it. If you don't mind me saying so, you are very tall and thin." She pronounced "thin" as "tin," with a French accent, and it took Kerry a few seconds to figure out what she was saying.

"Yeah, but I'm stronger than I look," she answered, not making eye contact. She could feel herself blushing beet red.

Yvette lifted her sunglasses off her face and examined Kerry as if she was a bug under a microscope. "Hmmm. If you say so. I'm not so sure."

CHAPTER 2

Yvette kicked off her sandals and picked her way up the strip of grass. Kerry, burdened with the largest of Yvette's packs, wallowed in the girl's wake.

"It's really buggy in here!" said Kerry.

"Bugs don't like me."

Well, that makes two million of us.

"Where's my room?"

"Honestly, I don't know. The boss didn't leave me a key. He said we'd be in the trailer but it's locked."

Yvette shrugged and kept moving toward the construction trailer. She turned the door handle of the end room right and left and pushed with her shoulder while turning hard. Open sesame.

"Everybody knows how to do that. Those locks never work; I don't know why they bother with them."

Well, I don't know how! Kerry felt panic rise in her throat. No locks working anywhere, not even on the bedroom door! She wasn't going to sleep for a minute in this place.

The room was about eight by ten feet, with dark, fake wood paneling. There was a cot on each side wall, with a matching dresser at the foot, and two closets flanked the door. Yvette ran a hand along the windowsill, checking for dust, and seemed satisfied. She bounced on the blue-and-white striped mattress and the cot squeaked. "Let's find your room. I hope you don't snore because these walls are paper thin." Kerry followed her outside and watched her break into the other rooms, each one bare of furniture.

"They expect us to share the same small space for the whole summer?" Kerry said.

Yvette frowned. In the bottom drawer of her dresser she found two sets of white sheets. She threw one set at Kerry and started making up the bed on the left side of the room. On the upper shelf in each closet was a gray wool army blanket wrapped in plastic. Yvette waited while Kerry wrestled with her bedding.

"If we make the furniture into an L-shape, it will give us more space," Yvette said.

"What about asking for another room?"

"You can if you like, but this is better than a tent, and that's how they'll think about it."

A tent? Kerry'd never slept in a tent in her life.

For the next five minutes the girls moved furniture, leaving a space for a makeshift table at the head of Yvette's bed. She upturned a cardboard box and covered it with a piece of leopard-print fabric pulled from the Holt's bag, as Kerry gazed on in amazement. She handed Kerry the end of a matching piece of drapery and together they stretched it along the top of the window—a perfect fit. Yvette fished around in her purse and came up with some finishing nails, which she banged into place with the heel of her shoe while Kerry held the fabric in place. They both stood back to admire the effect.

"You could almost do a jig in here," said Kerry.

Yvette dove one more time into the shopping bag. She tossed one throw pillow with a leopard and zebra pattern at Kerry and placed the other where the down pillow met the wool blanket.

"Cute," admitted Kerry.

Yvette lifted her shoulders and ran a hand through her cropped blonde hair. "It's better to achieve a balance."

Kerry rummaged through her duffel bag for her stuffed bear and leaned him up against the pillow. "I call him Rover because he goes everywhere with me."

"He looks happy camouflaged against the pillow. I was never allowed to have toy bears because we lived in the bush, and my *grand-maman* believed they gave children a missed message, since bears are wild and dangerous creatures, not meant for cuddling."

"Actually, it's 'mixed message,' but 'missed' sounds kind of poetic."

Each girl stretched out on her bed and looked up at the ceiling, the silence long and awkward between them. Kerry got out her phone and tried one more time. "I can't figure it out. This thing was working just fine in Toronto."

Yvette snorted. "I didn't even bring mine; the service is so bad up here. We can always go to the library to check our e-mail. They have strict rules about personal use at the department, so don't try it there."

"Omigod, I'm going to go mental!"

"There's always snail mail. It can be fun."

Kerry swung her legs to the floor and sat up. "I totally forgot. The boss, Mr. Harcourt, said we're supposed to go to the office—'the minute she gets here,' he said. He was pissed you were late."

"Lots of time." Yvette yawned and rolled over with her back to Kerry.

A minute later, Kerry could tell from Yvette's breathing that she was dead asleep. Kerry felt like pounding the walls. All that waiting and now this! She thumped down on her bed and grabbed the *Canadian Geographic Magazine* that her mom had pressed into her hand at the airport. She read for the tenth time the article on avoiding a cougar attack. She checked the little map showing the territory of the cougar in Ontario. There'd been unconfirmed sightings, nothing official, but now DNA samples of poop proved that cougars were here. What else lurked in the woods? Snakes? Wolves?

Kerry was about to shake Yvette awake when her partner yawned and stretched. "A little catnap is the best thing when you're tired; I learned that from my dad." Yvette reached into her day pack and set a round tin and cigarette papers on the bed and started rolling.

She does drugs? Oh my God! There's more than an ounce in that tin. She's going to deal *drugs from our room!*

When Yvette had a nice little pile of eight joints, she offered one to Kerry.

"I don't smoke weed."

Yvette laughed. "How old are you? It's a cigarette. I'm trying to quit so I roll my own."

Kerry was relieved. "Well, I don't smoke anything. Do you have to do that in here?"

"I wasn't going to, not unless you were a smoker too. Maybe this will help me to stop. How old are you?"

Kerry again ignored the question. "It's one o'clock; we'd better get going. The supervisor is really mad at you already."

Yvette checked her watch and opened her large pack. She dumped it on the bed and stacked the contents. First a pile of beige cargo pants and shorts. Then a larger stack of white shirts, some long-sleeved turtlenecks and the rest crisply ironed T-shirts. An assortment of light-colored hoodies and one pair of skinny 7 for All Mankind jeans that looked as if they cost the earth. She hung several faded plaid flannel shirts in the closet alongside a two-piece Gore-Tex rain suit and a Speedo bathing suit. Mitts, hats, and gloves went into the bottom drawer.

"We're going to need *mitts?*" Kerry could hear the shriek in her voice.

"Come mid-August, it's likely. And of course you have to wear light colors to keep the bugs away." As Yvette spoke, she set a fishing tackle box on the dresser and flipped the lid to reveal an array of beauty products, mostly from France. She applied Miss Dior lipstick while looking deep into the oval magnifying mirror resting on her dresser. She pinched her cheeks.

"You see, I have champagne tastes," she said. "And a beer budget. I'm lucky my aunt works at Holt's and gets a fifty percent discount. I'm looking forward to making a lot of money this summer. You too?"

Kerry nodded. On one thing they agreed—lots of money might make this all worth it. "I think we should get going."

Yvette stepped out of her shorts and stripped off her top in one motion. Dangling between her breasts were an Indian arrowhead and an animal tooth strung on a leather thong. She pulled on a white pair of jeans and a v-necked T-shirt that showed some cleavage and a lacy strap. She slipped her colored toes into wool work socks and into worn work boots that had pieces of duct tape capping the toes. She draped a muted gray-blue flannel shirt over her shoulders as if it were a dinner jacket and did a pirouette, admiring herself in the mirror and inviting Kerry's opinion.

"You look nice. Can we go now?"

But Yvette wasn't through. She searched through a side flap and dumped a handful of stuff on the bed. "Check out this windup flashlight emergency radio combo that doesn't need batteries. Amazing, eh? And this bug jacket. Did you bring a bug jacket?" She raised her arms and tugged what looked like forest green netting with cuffs over her head. "The hood zippers over the top of my head so I'm entirely covered down to my ass."

"So you don't have super-immunity against bugs?"

"You have to know that was a joke. You have never been up north in June?"

"I've never been up north. Period."

"Oh, man. Well, June is blackfly month. There are always mosquitoes and deer-flies if it's hot. Ever heard the saying 'I'm being eaten alive'?"

Kerry nodded.

"Well, you better believe it. There are many stories about people lost in the woods who go crazy because of the blackflies and bury themselves up to their necks to get away from them. The little buggers take pieces of meat out of you, especially behind the ears, the ankles, the neckline, waistbands, wherever they can sneak in. Kids are always getting the scabs infected. Sometimes you see them wrapped up in cheesecloth so they can play outside. They look like small white mummies sitting in the sandbox, with dribbles of blood here and there. June is the worst month up here."

Kerry felt completely useless and stupid. Her heart was racing so fast she could barely breathe. Her knee began to itch and she couldn't help scratching it. "I . . . I don't have the right gear, I mean, even my T-shirts are too dark. Maybe . . . I'd better go home."

"Maybe you should." Yvette paused for several seconds. *"Kidding!* You can probably borrow stuff from the office. Anyways, if it stays hot like this, the bugs won't last long." She took off her net jacket, rolled it up, and tucked it in the bottom of her chest of drawers. "Time to go."

"We're so late!"

Yvette tapped her watch. "The office staff are at dinner now. In the north, the offices close at noon so the workers can go home for a big meal. We have time to walk."

"Noon? My phone says it's almost two o'clock."

"Voyons, Kerry, don't you know we're an hour behind? We're in a different time zone from Toronto."

"A different time zone?" said Kerry. "More like a different planet!"

CHAPTER 3

Kerry walked gingerly along the highway into town, trying to keep up with Yvette but rapidly falling behind. She could see Yvette turning and walking backwards to check on her progress. Stabbing, needlelike pain traveled up and down her shins. She flapped her hands, riling the bugs. Yvette was out of sight now and Kerry limped faster. Finally Yvette waited for her to catch up.

"Sorry, uh, these boots are new," Kerry lied.

Yvette rolled her eyes and entered the office of the Department of Forestry and Parks. As no one was back from dinner yet, the receptionist showed the girls to the boss's office. Yvette headed straight for a coffeemaker in the corner.

"Coffee?" she asked.

"Thanks, no, I'm not a coffee drinker. I'm starving, though."

Yvette rummaged around in her pack and threw her a granola bar. "So, what *do* you drink?"

Kerry was confused. "I drink gallons of water when I'm working out."

Yvette laughed. "We have a winner here! I mean what kind of *booze* do you drink? And don't tell me something lame like Brandy Alexanders."

"I don't drink. I'm underage."

"Great, great!" Yvette rolled her *r*'s like a Scot. "So do you perhaps grow your own?"

"Very funny."

"Many things are illegal, you know," said Yvette. "Illegal, immoral, or fattening."

Kerry felt herself being surveyed from top to toe. She knew that she was tall, lanky, and flat as a board, and that she looked like a dancer, with her great turned-out boats for feet, and legs up to her neck. People were always telling her that her gray-blue eyes were expressive. She must look like a scared jackrabbit at the moment. She'd always had trouble with new people and situations, and Yvette was making her feel younger and smaller inside with every question. *Yvette has done everything! My life's been nothing but dance and homework. Thanks, Mom!* Kerry stared at the floor and waited for the next question she wouldn't be able to answer.

A man's voice boomed from the hall. "Oh God," Kerry said, "here he comes! He sounds mad."

"Relax," said Yvette, crossing her legs and shrugging off her flannel shirt. "Watch and learn." She sprawled one arm casually across the back of the empty chair beside her, striking a relaxed but powerful pose. When the supervisor shuffled in, filling the doorway with his stocky frame, the girls were rewarded by a startled look on his face.

Yvette waited until he'd folded himself in behind his metal desk before extending her hand to him. "How do you do? I'm Yvette Bernier and I've dislocated your schedule. Please permit me to apologize."

The supervisor sat back in his chair and swiveled from side to side while Yvette's outstretched hand hovered above the desk. Finally he took it. "Buzz Harcourt . . . and you're late. I've no intention of paying you girls for today. It's been a total write-off."

"No, please, that's not fair to Kerry, who arrived on time. I think you should reconsider her case, at least. I was unavoidably late because Air Canada lost my baggage. Perhaps it would be better to pay us as if this was a travel day?"

"I'll take that under advisement," muttered Harcourt. He shuffled through the papers on his desk. "You need to fill in these payroll and income tax forms. There's also a confidentiality document where you have to swear you won't give away any government secrets. You girls will be working ten days on and four days off, unless we drop you into a lake, in which case you'll work until the project's done. Then we'll arrange to pick you up. The job has a fancy title but all you're really going to do is dig test pits for septic systems and tell us where you find decent cottage sites."

Kerry felt her eyes bulge. *Dig? In Toronto they said I'd be writing reports. I can't do this!*

"Of course you pay overtime?" asked Yvette.

"There'll be no overtime. Ever. You'll work eight hours a day."

"Even if we're stuck in a tent in a place with nowhere to go, we'll be working without pay?" There was an edge to Yvette's voice now.

Harcourt put both hands on the desk and lifted himself partway out of the chair. "Listen, sweetie, if you don't want this job, I've got lots of local kids who'd love to make $14.50 an hour larking about on the lakes, looking for places for people to build a cottage."

Kerry kicked Yvette in the ankle. Yvette opened her mouth but closed it again, and they both turned their attention to the pile of paper. Yvette was reading slowly and carefully, while Kerry signed everything without reading it. When Yvette finished with the last form, Harcourt stood up impatiently. "I'll take you to the warehouse and you can start gathering your equipment. But all you'll really need is a shovel. As I said, you're going to do a lot of digging this summer."

Kerry finally found the nerve to speak up. "You've lost me. I thought we were working in the office. My mother said I'd be writing reports."

"Yeah, right." Harcourt held up a binder. "This here is the manual on how to fluffy up a cottage development report, according to the government's policy bozos in Toronto. Up here, the only thing we care about is the number of cottage sites you find that are capable of taking a septic system. You're going to have to dig a four-foot hole on every suitable site to see if you hit groundwater."

Yvette, eyes glazed, lifted her head. "Excuse me, sir. I have another question. Don't we have to be licensed to do that kind of work?"

The supervisor looked at her over his glasses. "You'll do what you're told," he said.

Yvette rummaged in her day pack for a notepad. She bit the cap off her pen and started writing.

"What're you doing?" Harcourt asked.

"I'm just making a note that I asked if we needed special training, and how you responded. I like to keep notes as things come up. I also noted that you don't want to pay us for today even though it's just after dinner now. I did this job last year in Chapleau, so I know what to expect."

It was so quiet in the room that Kerry could hear a fly committing suicide inside the overhead light fixture.

"Listen, missy, I won't be intimidated." Harcourt turned his attention to Kerry. "And you. Do I look like a babysitter, here? What are you, sixteen?"

"Seventeen," Kerry whispered.

"Great. You have a driver's license and a boating permit?"

She nodded.

"Well, I don't know who you know in the government to have landed this job. Maybe you have friends in Ottawa? You speak Frog, right?"

"I'm the one who speaks French," Yvette said. "My father was French."

"Was?"

"He's deceased."

There was no murmur of condolence from Buzz. He finished witnessing the confidentiality forms and motioned them to follow him. On the way to the warehouse, he introduced them to other staff only when someone was bearing down on them in the hallway. Each time, he'd say, "These are the two summer students from down east, the ones who are going to look for cottage sites for the Sale/Lease program." As there was never any exchange of names, Yvette properly introduced herself and Kerry, making sure that everyone knew that she was no "down-easterner"; she'd been born in Winnipeg and brought up in Labrador, and had lived in Northern Quebec and then in Cornwall, Ontario.

The concrete-block warehouse by the lake was stacked from floor to ceiling with racks of equipment, including outboard motors, pumps, and canoe packs. Kerry fingered the nozzle of a fire hose that had come loose from its coil.

"Don't touch that stuff," Harcourt said, pushing her away. "It belongs to Forestry. Take what you need from the Parks side only. Everything is numbered and tagged and you log it out in this book."

"Sounds easy enough." Kerry gave him a bright smile. "Are there any women firefighters here?" she asked, trying to make polite conversation.

"What kind of dumb-ass question is that? Haven't you heard we got a quota system here? Those assholes in Toronto deny it, saying it's all about merit, but don't you believe it. We get stuck with broads. But we don't have any right now. Good thing, too. Do you think you could walk around all day with a seventy-five-pound pack on your back? *Could you?*"

Kerry stepped back as if she'd been hit, feeling the sting of tears in her eyes. She willed herself not to blink. Yvette caught her eye and made a farting sound with her mouth on the back of her arm, and it was all Kerry could do to keep from bursting out laughing. Yvette turned her back to the supervisor and started rummaging through sleeping bags. "These arctic bags are perfect. Is our boat docked somewhere?"

"It's in the yard." He motioned for them to follow him out to where all manner of boats were turned upside down on the grass, like turtles basking in the sun. Harcourt headed to the back fence and pointed to a steel, flat-bottomed boat rusting along its seams.

Kerry watched while Yvette nudged it with her toe. "Well, she looks sturdy enough," she said, "but it's going to take a lot of horsepower to get her plowing through the water. Where'd you hide the trailer?"

He sighed and rolled his eyes. "Lady, there is no trailer. You'll just have to lift with your knees like the rest of us and heave it into the back of the truck."

"Come on, that thing's a tank. It's not possible for two girls to lift it. What about this little aluminum one? It looks perfect."

"Belongs to Forestry. Listen, if this job is too tough for you, I'm sure they have something cushier in Toronto."

Yvette narrowed her eyes and stepped toward him. "I'm a bit confused, Monsieur Harcourt. Maybe it was missing in my file, but I'm going into second-year civil engineering at Waterloo. I know my way around boats."

"We do things different here. And you sure don't look like any kind of engineer I've ever seen."

"I think we'll be okay to handle the boat, Mr. Harcourt," Kerry said hastily. "But do we get a phone in case we have an emergency out on the lake? You know, if we run out of gas or something?"

He laughed. "You see all this rock? Cell phones are pretty much useless around here. So the answer is no, you won't get a phone."

"Hang on, please," Yvette said. "It's a good question.

We need a radio when we're out in the field—you know, the kind the fire crews use."

"There are no radios or satellite phones available."

"I saw a whole warehouse full of them a minute ago."

"That stuff is for Forestry and you can't touch it. I don't have a budget for phones for summer students and—"

"Let me get this straight," Kerry said. "You're sending us out in the bush for ten days or maybe more, hundreds of miles away, without any way of communicating with anyone?"

"Correct. That's my policy."

Yvette fished in her bag for her little notebook and wrote furiously, saying under her breath, "No trailer . . . no radio . . ."

Harcourt grinned and jangled a set of keys. "Do I look like I'm worried? Your chariot awaits, girls." He tossed the keys high above Kerry's head but she caught them. "There's a red Dodge pickup truck parked out front. It's for business use only. It's new and a rental, so go easy on it. Got it?"

Kerry nodded and Harcourt stomped away. When he rounded the corner, Yvette kicked the steel boat with her steel-toed boots. The sound reverberated but she didn't make a dent. Kerry grabbed the rope and gave the boat a tug, but it was immovable.

"We need to stay as far away from that guy as possible. He's a jerk," Yvette said.

"I don't see how we can, if he's our boss. I wonder what 'Buzz' stands for."

Yvette snorted. "How about 'Buzz Off'?"

CHAPTER 4

When they went out to the truck, Yvette took charge. "I'll teach you how to do a circle check." She found a logbook in the glove compartment and marked down the starting mileage, then walked around the truck checking for dents and scratches. "Tell me if the taillights and the headlights are working," she called from inside the cab. Kerry watched while Yvette tested the wipers and adjusted the mirrors. She honked twice, pulled out, and let Kerry in. When they got back to the bunkhouse, it appeared they were still the only ones home.

"I'm exhausted," said Kerry. "I feel like I've been working for a week and it's only the first day."

"It's because everything is new. Tomorrow will be worse and then it'll get better. Don't you find that with a new job? Oops, sorry, this is probably the first job you've ever had."

Kerry nodded. "I'm so lucky to get an asshole for a supervisor!"

"He's just a little man trying to be a big toad in a small pond . . ."

Kerry choked with laughter. "You mean a big *frog!*"

"On the first day, it's important to show him who's really the boss. You have to stand up to him and not let him push you around. It's like dogs pissing on fire hydrants, and I'm the biggest, baddest dog in the park!"

Kerry shook her head, trying not to imagine Yvette peeing on hydrants. But thank God that she seemed to know everything about everything. All of a sudden, the clench in Kerry's stomach was gone. "I'm hungry," she said.

Yvette opened a bag of almonds with her teeth and passed it to Kerry. "The guys will be here pretty soon. Supper's at five-thirty. We're having chicken tonight, no?"

Kerry sniffed the air. She hadn't even noticed that yummy smell until Yvette pointed it out. Now she needed something to take her mind off her growling stomach. "Um—do you have any pictures of your family?"

"Sure." Yvette reached into her pack and tossed Kerry a small album. The front had a picture of Audrey Hepburn smoking a cigarette in an elegant cigarette holder. Kerry opened the book up to the first page.

"That's me," said Yvette, "the one in the big boot."

Kerry brought the photo up to her nose to get a better look at the blonde, curly-haired kid in a sunsuit, standing in a hip wader up to her waist.

"Maman was afraid it would fill up with water and I'd drown."

"Great smile," said Kerry. "Like you took a puck in the mouth."

"Could I ever spit water out that gap, from one side of the creek to the other. That's why I caught so many fish. They were attracted to the spit, and when they got bored of spit, they went for the worm."

"Who took the picture?"

"Papa. He propped me up in the boot, let me go for a second, and then snapped it. Of course, I didn't really catch any fish. He'd hook one, pass me the rod, and guess what?—my fish!"

"Sounds like fun."

"The best fun. He'd carry me into the house sound asleep in his arms, wrapped up in his scratchy red wool sweater with the arms tied tight. I loved that sweater." She fell silent, then added, "Maman pitched it in the garbage after he died, along with everything else except those flannel shirts—they were hanging on a hook in the garage. For a year I slept with the smell of Papa under my pillow, and then in the morning I'd hide the shirts under the mattress. But finally she found them and washed him away." She cleared her throat and continued, "Those shirts, a couple of pictures, his hard hat, and this necklace are just about all I've got."

Kerry leaned in for a closer look at a picture of Yvette's dad and linked her arm through Yvette's. She turned to the next page, a photo of Yvette in a spaghetti-strap dress hanging onto the arm of a drop-dead gorgeous guy in a tuxedo.

"He's cute. Is that your brother?"

"My last boyfriend. He was twenty-seven, with a good job at the bank and a car and a house."

"How old are you, there?"

"Let's see. I'm nineteen now, so seventeen, about your age. He was divorced and Maman didn't like him because of that. What about you? Do you have a boyfriend?"

Yvette looked so confident in the picture. Kerry

couldn't imagine talking to a man ten years older than herself, let alone dating him. "Me? Not at the moment." "Never" would have been more truthful. "I'm too busy," she said, repeating the reason her mother had drummed into her brain.

"Well, we'll have lots of chances this summer. Firefighters are big and handsome guys."

Kerry closed the book. They had the whole summer to get to the next picture. Sitting next to Yvette, she felt twelve and a half.

Without warning, the camp exploded with the sound of pickup trucks skidding on gravel. There was shouting and hooting as car doors slammed. Loud voices teased and taunted. Radios and CD players competed and the whole clearing throbbed with a bass beat. When Kerry peered through the glass porthole in the door, she saw that the clearing was alive with guys, some of them wearing orange coveralls held up by shoulder straps. They all seemed tall and powerful, with strong muscles bulging under tight T-shirts.

"There are so many. I wonder if we'll have to eat in two sittings," said Yvette.

A middle-aged woman opened the screen door to the cookhouse and clanged a metal triangle announcing supper. The call jangled through the clearing, sending the whiskey jacks flying for cover. The bunkhouse door flew open and a stream of guys ran to the cookhouse, the screen door thwacking open and shut, open and shut, until silence reigned again.

"Well, I guess that answers my question. We better get in there or there won't be anything left." Yvette brushed her hair and applied new lipstick. Kerry threw on a sweatshirt that matched her eyes.

"Ready, Kerry?"

Kerry smiled weakly. Thank heavens she had a partner. She'd rather starve to death than walk into a roomful of strange guys. Her hands began to shake and she had a hard time locking the trailer door. Yvette strolled across the clearing and yanked open the screen door. They had taken only two strides inside when the room went dead quiet. Kerry felt the nerves up and down her spine prickle as twenty pairs of eyes stared at her. Yvette kept going, the heels of her boots sounding hollow on the plywood floor. Then she stopped and Kerry crashed into her. What was Yvette doing? Was she going to *speak* to them? Kerry wanted to run back out that door.

"It's so sad you've never seen girls before," Yvette announced. "I think you've been in the bush too long. You, yes you, the one with the hairy beard—close your mouth. Permit me to introduce my friend Kerry. My name is Yvette and we are your cottage development technicians for the summer. I hope you've left us something to eat because we are growing girls."

The room erupted in good-natured laughter and Yvette bowed to the crowd. But Kerry noticed a sheen of perspiration above her partner's lip, so maybe this wasn't as easy as she made it appear.

Yvette smiled at the cook's helper behind a steam table of stainless steel pots. "I'll have half of everything. Hold the gravy, and is there salad? Thanks, I can serve myself."

Kerry moved quickly to take her place. "I'll have the same, please. Smells fantastic."

Yvette took her tray and searched the room for a suitable spot, and some of the guys at the front table shuffled along the bench to make room for them. Kerry couldn't plunk her tray down fast enough. She perched on the bench across from Yvette and, head down, started to eat. She wasn't listening to Yvette's chirpy patter, although she managed to murmur "ah-huh" and "oh, no" in all the right places.

In a low voice, Yvette said, "Kerry, slow down."

"Oh—right." She hadn't been aware that she was shoveling her food. It was a nervous habit, eating so fast. Besides, the supper was surprisingly good. There was pork roast with stuffing, not chicken, real mashed potatoes with a blob of melted butter, not margarine, and sides of spaghetti, peas, and carrots that weren't the least bit mushy.

"This is amazing," she said to Yvette.

"Food is everything in the bush. It's what these guys look forward to all day. If you're not careful, you'll gain twenty-five pounds this summer."

With visions of a competition dress that wouldn't zip up, and her mother's critical comments, Kerry put her fork down. Then she picked it up again. Not worrying about her weight for one night wouldn't hurt. And there had to be some compensation for being banished to this place!

The guys returned their trays and were waiting in orderly fashion for coffee and lemon meringue pie or gooey butter tarts, or both. Kerry gaped. "Two desserts? The most I get at home is fruit salad. Mom says desserts are just empty calories."

Yvette rose from her seat and headed for the salad bar. Kerry felt panic flutter from her stomach to her throat, and even though she wasn't hungry, she got up and followed her. A guy with white-blond hair and twinkly blue eyes came up behind her. "Which of you two lovely women is the dancer who's going into kine-siology this fall?"

Yvette and Kerry looked at each other. "The dancer? That'd be me," said Kerry. "How'd you know?"

"We have our ways. Most of what we need to know is written on the men's room wall. I'm Didier. I know dancing isn't really a sport or anything, but a couple of us guys go for a jog in the evening before going to the hotel for drinks. You're welcome to come with us."

"Thanks," said Kerry. "I'd like to, but I have pretty bad shin splints and I have to take it easy."

Didier looked sympathetic, making him even more gorgeous. "Whenever you're up for it."

Yvette returned to the table with a plate heaped with salad, no dressing, and two cubes of cheddar cheese. She frowned at the butter tart and the slice of lemon meringue pie on Kerry's plate. "Well, I can see you're not anorexic. But you didn't tell me you were injured, or that you're a dancer. What kind of a dancer?"

"Irish. And I'm fine, but I'm not good enough to com-pete for the rest of the season."

"Like Riverdance?"

Kerry nodded. "I've been doing it since I was a kid. It's been my whole life up until now."

"Ah-hahh, now I get it. Shin splints—that's some kind of muscle thing, isn't it? I hope your legs are strong enough for fieldwork. It's not safe to go into the bush if you're not healthy. Did you mention this to Buzz?"

Kerry took a mouthful of butter tart and syrup dribbled down her chin. "Jeez, Yvette, I'm new but I'm not stupid. Really, I'm okay. I just can't dance at the moment and my mother didn't want me hanging around if I couldn't compete. She's obsessed with winning. Besides, I don't see how shin splints are going to stop me from riding around in a boat." As she spoke, the metal teapot she was using dribbled puddles of golden tea on the table, and Yvette mopped it up with her paper serviette. "Seriously, they told me I'd be working in an office, otherwise I'd never have taken this job. My mother would freak if she knew what's going on—which actually makes it almost worth it. You don't know me yet, but I'm no quitter. I'll prove it to you." *Wow, where did that come from?* Kerry thought, but she realized that she meant every word.

"We'll see. We have to work as a team, you know? Working in the bush isn't an individual thing. You have to rely on your buddy. I have this thing about safety. For me, safety comes first." Yvette wiggled in her seat, humming tunelessly while tapping her fingers against her coffee mug, looking jumpy.

A couple of guys were lighting up cigarettes. "I don't know why I'm surprised they can smoke in here. I guess it's kind of their residence," Kerry said. "Look, if you want a smoke all that badly, why don't you just have one?"

Yvette fished around in the bottom of her pack and came up with a slightly bent, somewhat untwisted "roll your own." Before she had a chance to get out her pink Bic lighter, Didier lit her cigarette with a wooden match.

"*Merci beaucoup.*"

"When do you girls go out on the lakes?"

Yvette blew a long breath of smoke skyward. "Tomorrow. I like to do a dry run to test the equipment before we go on a big trip."

"Good idea. I'm the crew boss of one of the fire units, and I'd be happy to answer any questions you have. Most of the guys you see are in the forestry program at Lakehead. This is my third summer here."

"Lucky," said Kerry. It was just one word but it brought her into the conversation. *If only I had more experience with guys,* she thought.

"Yep, it's pretty nice up here, especially in the summer, but it's hard to make a buck in winter. Do you know where you're headed tomorrow?"

"Not a clue," Yvette said.

"There are some good spots north of here, off this highway." Didier leaned over and flipped the plasticized Ontario road map off the wall and set it down on the table between them. "There's a put-in on Trout Lake and another one just here."

"They'd better be easy ones because we've got a pig of a boat without a trailer," said Kerry. "And a pig of a boss."

"Ah, Harcourt. He flunked out of Waterloo engineering fifteen years ago and was lucky to land a job, so he can't be happy with Yvette here rubbing it in his face."

"Wow, you're well-informed," said Yvette. "I can't help it if engineering kind of runs in our family."

"Well, I have a tip for you girls. Stay on his good side if you don't want to be on the receiving end of a sore paw. Buzz can be as grouchy as a bear."

"What do you mean?" Kerry's heart thumped out of her chest at the prospect of the supervisor hitting her. But nothing would surprise her with that guy.

Didier ignored her and yelled at a burly guy across the room, "Hey, Aubrey, you know this lake. Where should these girls put in? Hey girls, meet Aubrey, nickname the Bear Whisperer."

Kerry shook hands, a firm, dry handshake, with a guy who looked at her with brown eyes so deep she thought she might fall in. "Why do they call you the Bear Whisperer?"

Aubrey chuckled. "I guess because I'm Metis and I study bear behavior. Right now I'm a fire crew boss, but I'd like to be a conservation officer one day."

"Where's the best place to launch our boat?" Yvette interrupted.

Aubrey leaned over the map. "There's rapids at the outlet of this river, so avoid that. I'd suggest the lower end of the lake beside this tourist camp."

Didier and Aubrey couldn't be more different, physically. Kerry tried hard not to stare. *One dark, one bright white, but both so big and muscled. Didier is movie-star hot. Aubrey is . . . interesting with that cleft chin. Is it my imagination, or does Yvette not like Aubrey at all?*

Yvette was fumbling for her lighter, and Aubrey leaned over and relit her mangled cigarette. She didn't bother to thank him.

"Well, good luck tomorrow. It's supposed to be a windy day so there could be quite a chop, so take care," Didier said. "Oh, I forgot. You're invited to the bunkhouse for drinks tonight at seven-thirty. I know it's early, but we have to work tomorrow."

"I'll walk you back to your trailer," Aubrey offered.

"You don't have to," said Yvette.

"I know, but it's no problem." He held the door for the girls, and Kerry was struck by his height and quiet strength as she walked past him. She'd never met anyone like him, so reserved but so confident.

When they reached the trailer, Aubrey leaned close and lowered his voice. "Make sure you lock your doors at night. We've had some funny things go missing around this camp, and at the office."

"No one mentioned this," said Yvette.

"No one wants to admit there's a problem."

"What kind of things?" Kerry's voice sounded wobbly to her own ears.

"Gas cans. Flares. A radio. Barbecue lighters. Even a brand new Sea-Doo. Tons of stuff."

When they got back to their room, Yvette pulled her large pack from under her bed and braced it in front of the door. She hung her boots over the door handle. "I need a nap before tonight. This way, if they come through this booby trap, at least we'll hear them. Maybe then we won't show up under the heading of 'stuff' that goes missing."

"You mean *I'll* hear them. I'll bet you can sleep through anything," said Kerry.

"I sleep like the murdered."

"You mean the *dead*."

"*Exactement.*"

Kerry crawled into bed but her mind kept racing over all the things that had happened in just one day. She could hardly believe she'd left home just yesterday. She felt as if she'd been here a week. *I'm not sure I'll be able to last. I've never met people like this before—especially Yvette. I wonder what Mom and Dad are doing, and if they miss me. . . .*

"Hey, Yvette, how can you stand it? I'm going mental not talking to my friends, let alone my family. It feels so weird being cut off like this."

"I'm used to it. Love the ones you're with, as they say. Summer jobs up here are intense, and then you go back to your normal life. Now, have a nap or you'll never be able to last tonight."

"Yes, Mom." Kerry wadded her thin pillow under her neck and hugged Rover, burying her face in his raggedy fur.

Normal? I haven't got a clue what normal means anymore.

CHAPTER 5

Yvette woke up first and went out. She came bounding back up the steps of the trailer, smelling of cigarette smoke. "Someone sent you a letter even before you left home!"

"That would be my mother." Kerry yawned and fired the envelope into the bottom drawer of the dresser.

"Aren't you going to open it?"

"She's a head case," Kerry sighed. "And she's the one who sent me here. If I can't dance, I'm useless. But now she's probably had second thoughts, probably expects me to dump this job and start dancing again, no matter what the doctor says."

"Oh, she's one of those pushy backstage moms. . . ."

"She frames the ribbons I win and hangs them in the rec room beside my trophies. She's always at my poor dad to put up more shelving. There's a lot of pressure on me to win. She's a freaking perfectionist about everything, even how I glue my socks—"

"You glue your socks?"

"With surgical glue, so they don't fall down when I compete. Points off if your socks fall down. She even

38

controls what wig I wear. One day I'm Lady Gaga in curls, and the next day I'm a redhead. I just got a flashy new competition dress, and it must be killing her that I can't wear it."

"Are you her only kid?" Kerry nodded, her teeth clenched. "She must really miss you. Is this the first time you're away from home?"

"Yeah. So pathetic."

Yvette picked at her nails. "I used to get so fed up with my dad. Sometimes he pissed me off and I'd punish him by not speaking to him. But now he's gone, and I can't take that back."

"It's not the same thing."

"She obviously loves—"

"She weighs my *food!* Every stupid calorie. She pinches my waist and says I'm getting fat."

Yvette sucked in a long, slow breath. "Okay then. Well, I think you look fabulous. You just don't know it yet."

"She made my whole life revolve around dancing. So now that I can't do it, I feel like crap."

"Well, if you dance the way you eat, you must be something. You're like a hungry greyhound puppy, all long legs and so geeky you don't know what to do with yourself."

Kerry couldn't help laughing. "You mean *gawky.*"

The two girls scrambled to get ready. Kerry rinsed the bug juice out of her hair and put on a pair of jeans, a red tank top, and running shoes. Yvette dressed similarly, but somehow the effect was entirely different. Her tank top was more coral than red, with a plunging neckline. She tucked it into the waist of black capris accentuated with a white leather belt. Instead of runners, she wore coral flip-flops and a two-minute spray of Deep Woods Off up to her knees. Then she added a silver ankle bracelet, like a charm bracelet on drugs.

"You like it?" she asked. "These little things are from my father's fishing box. Don't worry, I clipped off the hooks. This yellow one was his favorite trout-fishing fly. This is a sinker. This fish tooth already had a hole in it. You can recognize a plastic worm, except it's lime green, and these are supposed to be fish eggs. A good way to start a conversation, no?"

Kerry laughed. "A good way to make the guys look at your ankles. . . ." *Watch and learn,* she thought, feeling like an ugly stepsister.

"*Voilà.* This will make us *very* popular." Yvette pulled out a big liquor bottle. "It's tequila from Mexico. Strong stuff! Try some."

"I'll pass," Kerry said quickly. "I've never had hard liquor."

"Come on," Yvette teased. "You have to start sometime. *Ç'est l'fun!*"

Kerry lay in bed. The bed seemed to be tilting, and she felt as if she were hovering above her own body, looking down. She sat bolt upright—*Ow, my head!*—as her stomach lurched and hot acid gushed up into her throat. She stumbled to the door and just made it to the porch before a disgusting mix of tequila and supper spewed up and landed at the base of a pine tree. Her hair stank and her breath stank as she vomited again and again.

She staggered along the path to the stream behind the trailer, knelt down and lost her balance, and almost toppled off the rock. She lay on her stomach, cool granite against her cheek, and sluiced water on her face. It had been a long time since she'd barfed, and she'd forgotten how really barfie it was. She clambered up and stumbled to the washroom and had a hot, soapy shower in the dark, by the glow of a flashlight, so the guys couldn't see in. *See, I remembered. I'm not that drunk.* "Whoopsie!" A third of the shampoo spilled into her hand and dripped between her fingers. She smeared shampoo all over her body and let it rinse away, and then wrapped herself in Yvette's terrycloth bathrobe. She flipped on the lights, fumbled through her bag, and took two aspirin with about a gallon of water. Back in the trailer, she changed into a new t-shirt and crawled into bed. Yvette didn't even know she'd been gone.

Had she really danced with Aubrey or was it a dream? She touched her cheek and thought she could still feel the warm flannel of his shirt, soft as the nightie her Irish grandma had given her when she was six. Her back felt weak where he'd placed his hand. Her head was dizzy as she recalled resting it on his shoulder, her light brown hair mixing with his black hair. The boy could dance! Her feet had barely touched the ground.

She must have fallen asleep, because the next thing she knew was the smell of coffee and bacon. She crawled to a standing position on her bed and peeked out the window. Maybe she could dash into the cookhouse for a jug of water and a couple of coffees, and slap together a bacon and tomato sandwich for Yvette, without running into anyone. Oh, and she could get her some chocolate milk. Yvette didn't look as if she was getting up till noon, not without help, anyway. Kerry tied her hair in a red bandanna and decided to skip brushing her teeth until after breakfast. She had her hand on the screen door of the cookhouse when Didier hailed her.

"Was that you I saw dancin' last night like a rock star?"

She bristled. "I'm not supposed to dance."

"I could have sworn you were dancing with Chief Two-Beers. You were all over him."

Kerry's mind raced. Should she deny it? It was none of Didier's business. *Omigod. It was Didier who kept feeding me coolers. What did I say to him? I remember a lot of questions about me, about Yvette, in exchange for more drinks. Very personal stuff about why I liked Aubrey and why he didn't.*

"I can't dance." Kerry charged up to the front of the canteen and grabbed a tray. Of course Didier knew she'd danced with Aubrey. He and Yvette had been on the dance floor, making a game of bumping into them. She poured two glasses of chocolate milk, added a bowl of granola and the fixings for a bacon and tomato sandwich, and grabbed one black coffee.

Inside the trailer, she set the coffee down on Yvette's dresser and wafted the steam in her direction. "Wakey, wakey."

Yvette groaned.

"Have some chocolate milk; it's the best thing for a hangover," said Kerry.

"How would you know?" Yvette's voice sounded fuzzy.

"It's my dad's trick. On New Year's Day, after his annual bender, he puts on his party hat, drinks chocolate milk, and vacuums so my mother won't get mad at him. It's very cute."

Kerry supported Yvette while she took a long slurp. When Yvette flopped back down on the bed, she was already fast asleep.

"Ah, crap. Yvette, I feel like crap, too, but we have to show up for work. I'll go gas up the truck and get the stuff." Yvette pulled the pillow over her head.

Well, it's still early and I don't feel so great myself. Maybe a little walk will help. Kerry rifled through Yvette's dresser drawers for a can of bear repellent and shoved it in her back pocket. Yesterday she wouldn't have ventured out on her own, but something had changed overnight. She was getting used to this place. And those guys from Lakehead weren't all that scary when you got to know them. Starting with Didier. And Aubrey—she didn't know what to think about Aubrey. He was polite, walking the girls home last night and taking Yvette's lighter out of her hand to light her cigarette. But he seemed awfully quiet.

She used the stairs and railing of the trailer to stretch her muscles, especially her hamstrings. Then, beginning with a slow walk and building the pace, she turned north on the highway. There was a good breeze, and the bugs were nowhere to be found.

The trees looked delicate in the early morning light, with soft, bright green new growth at the end of each branch. Birds flitted in and out of the bushes that edged the highway, traveling with her and keeping her company. The sandy shoulder was soft to the foot and she fell into an even pace. She heard the low drone of a plane in the sky, then the *wappa, wappa* of a helicopter, and counted one floatplane and three helicopters following the highway northward. One of the pilots dipped low and waved at her, and Kerry waved back, making a peace sign.

Uh-oh, last night was coming back to her. A moment when she was dancing with Aubrey, and some of his fire crew, who called him Chief Two-Beers, told him to make love, not war. She remembered how his spine had stiffened, the set of his half-closed eyes, and then his arm thrusting above her head, his fingers forming a v, and him firmly saying, "Peace." She'd had her mouth open, ready to say something caustic. *Who did these people think they were, talking to their boss like that?* He'd pulled her to him and muffled her words against his chest. She'd felt the perspiration through his shirt. "Shh, let it go, they're drunk. It doesn't matter," he'd said.

But it mattered to her.

The sun was getting higher, and as Kerry crested a hill she cupped her eyes to get a better look at the sky. There was a hazy ring around the sun, like the rings of Saturn. "How weird is that!" She checked her heart rate and crossed the road to face any oncoming traffic, and began to retrace her steps. She'd gone as far as the garbage dump when gray-white flakes of ash rained down from the sky. *I can't believe they're allowed to burn garbage up here,* she thought. *I'm going to put in a report that burning garbage shouldn't be allowed.*

She was walking home, holding her hands palm up, catching powdery bits of ash like snowflakes, when a familiar green and white truck barreled over the rise. Didier stood on his brakes to bring the crew cab to a tire-screeching halt.

"What's going on?" Kerry asked.

"A big smoker thirty miles north of here. Don't look so stunned; you're covered in ash. It started on the island in Trout Lake, probably set by campers. Anyway, you'd better hustle. Harcourt's looking for you."

"Why?"

He put the truck in gear. "You'll find out."

Now what have I done? she thought. *We're not late yet.*

She tried to hurry but her shins were stinging. She stopped, bent at the waist, and rubbed down her legs. When she stood up a black bear, not twenty-five yards away, was loping down the middle of the road toward town. Her heart pounded out of her chest but the bear didn't appear to be any threat. When she caught up to the spot where she thought it had gone back into the bush, she started to run. She kept running until she reached the camp, only pausing to look over her shoulder.

When she got there, Harcourt was in his car, and he leaned on the horn. "I've been waiting for you for half an hour," he snapped. "You should tell people where you're going. I already spoke to your partner and she's getting ready to go."

"What's the rush? It's not even seven."

"A big fire's been burning all night and it's up to two hundred acres. We need some cooks on site by noon, and you've been volunteered."

"You're kidding, right? I don't know the first thing about cooking."

"Well, you better be a quick learner, because you're going. There'll be a plane at the dock in half an hour. Pack for about a week; we don't have a clue how long this will last. I've never seen it so hot and dry this early in the season."

"Gosh, Mr. Harcourt, I think you'd better get somebody else."

He lifted his sunglasses and parked them on his forehead. "Girl, you're not getting this, are you? You don't have a choice. Now that you've signed on, it's like being in the army. We tell you where to go and you go. That's it. We got legislation that gives us authority to conscript anybody and anything when there's a fire, but we start with our own staff. You are now a cook and there's nothing you can do about it. Got it?" Kerry moved away from his car. "And you'd better damn well be on time for the plane. If you're late, I'll dock you a week's pay, I swear I will."

Kerry choked on the dust plume kicked up as Harcourt's car shuddered down the lane. "You're such a jerk," she said, not caring who heard her.

She found the trailer unlocked and Yvette curled up in bed, her knees hugging her chest. Kerry nudged her shoulder, and when that didn't work she flicked on the overhead light. Yvette threw an arm over her eyes, motioning Kerry away with her other hand.

"Stop messing, Yvette. I'm not happy about being a cook either, but I don't see how we can get out of it."

Yvette sat bolt upright in bed, clinging to the blankets and shaking. "I'm not going." Her voice was barely audible. "I can't fly."

"What do you mean, you can't fly? Are you sick? I don't get it. Oh, you don't *like* flying? But you flew to get here."

Yvette shook her head. "No, *you* flew here. I took the bus for two stinking days. I was very clear to ask, and the personnel woman in Toronto said this job didn't include flying. I even wrote it down on the first page of my notebook."

Kerry sat on the bed beside her and took her hand. "Are you afraid of flying?"

"I promised Maman I wouldn't fly. Just so you know, my papa was killed in a small plane crash, flown by a drunk and unlicensed pilot. I promised her I'd never set foot in one of those things. Never ever. I won't do it."

Kerry thought she was going to be sick. No way she was going if Yvette didn't go. *Not alone. I don't know the first thing about cooking. Or camping. Or anything!* "Just get dressed." She started packing for both of them. "We'll figure something out."

"Kerry, listen to me. If I break my word, something dreadful will happen. It's the same feeling I had the morning Papa left for Quebec. I feel something anonymous."

"Huh? Something—something *ominous?*" Kerry pulled the drawstring tight around her sleeping bag. "Let's go. You can tell me about it on the way."

PART 2

Base Camp Number One

June 28–30

CHAPTER 6

Kerry took the wheel and Yvette rode shotgun into town. Immediately upon buckling up her seatbelt, she put a cigarette in her mouth and searched her day pack.

"*Maudite marde.* Where's my lighter? Have you seen my lighter? I hope I didn't lose it. I've had it for a long time, and they don't come in that hot pink anymore."

"I saw you with it at the party, I think," Kerry leaned forward and pushed in the cigarette lighter. Yvette sucked hard on her cigarette and blew smoke out the window.

"See, my bad luck has started. Losing my little Bic is a sign. I don't know what I should do. The overtime would be fantastic, but I promised Maman I wouldn't fly."

Kerry chewed on her lower lip and kept driving. When they reached the office, they found the yard crawling with staffers, and had to pick their way around hoses, pumps, and canvas tents. A yellow floatplane tugged on its ropes at the end of the dock, bobbing on the waves like a bathtub toy. "It looks so little," Kerry said.

Yvette squinted at the plane. "Actually it's decent-sized—it's a Beaver, likely operated by the department and not a private contractor. That's a good thing. At least they have safety standards. Things would have been different if my dad had been flying in a government plane."

Kerry shrugged into her pack and hugged her sleeping bag to her chest, but Yvette left her gear in the back of the truck. They walked to the edge of the lake and watched the pilot's every move. He'd laid all the cargo on the dock in order, from heaviest to lightest.

"I need to see his eyeballs," said Yvette.

The pilot looked up when their boots sounded on the dock. He was tall and broad-shouldered. Kerry thought he looked like a cop in his aviator glasses, but then he whipped them off and walked toward them with a big grin of welcome. He held out his hand to each in turn and she noted his firm and confident handshake. "Hi, ladies, Matthew Stanowski. A perfect day for flying, except for the fire, of course. Sure glad you travel light." He turned to Yvette. "Now don't get me wrong, but I think you've gone a bit *under*board. I've got room for your stuff."

"Thanks, but I'm not going with you."

"Really? I was told I'd be taking two girls and a Buzz Harcourt. Do you know how big he is?"

"He's short and lumpy," said Yvette. "I'd say he weighs about two hundred and fifty or so."

"So it's two of you for one of him. That could balance out nicely."

"You weren't listening. I'm not going, and that's final."

Matthew looked at Kerry for an explanation. She shrugged. "Yvette doesn't fly. They told her in Toronto she wouldn't have to."

Matthew leaned down to look into Yvette's eyes as if she were a scared little kid. "Okay, I understand how you feel. What can I do to change your mind?"

"Nothing. Oh, I don't know. Listen, have you got a match? I can't find my lighter."

Matthew reached deep into his pocket and handed her a pack of matches. "Keep it." He turned back to Kerry, giving her a cargo list and a pen. "I could use your help."

Kerry looked at all the cargo on the dock. It seemed like too much stuff for such a small plane. How was it ever going to get off the ground? Meanwhile, Yvette lit her cigarette, stomped to the end of the dock, and walked along the beach until she ran out of sand. She plunked down on a rock and scanned the water, tugging on her necklace as if she might yank it off.

"Sorry, Matthew, I have to go and see how my partner's doing. If she doesn't go, neither do I." Kerry clumped down the dock after Yvette.

"You okay?" Yvette shrugged and Kerry took a deep breath. "What would your papa do in a situation like this?"

"That's easy. He'd fly, never thinking about what could happen. But I . . . I swore to Maman, on the health of my unborn children, that I'd keep my two feet on the ground." She reached for another smoke, and then cupped her hands around a match. "And Maman won't survive if something happens to me. She's only now beginning to sleep, after a year. Papa would say lightning doesn't strike twice, almost never. But Kerry, what if crashing is my fate, too?"

Kerry wrapped an arm around her shoulders.

"And how would she cope with the little kids without me? Stéphane and Chantal fight all the time, and Danielle and Justin, the twins—well, two isn't a good age."

Kerry sighed. "I'm not good at this kind of stuff. I don't know what to say."

Yvette looked back at the plane, and the pilot loading the gear. "That fire—it's going to be rolling with all this wind. I don't know. . . ."

"Come on, Yvette. Let's go."

Reluctantly Yvette got up, and they walked back to the dock.

"May I see your license, if you don't mind?" Yvette said to the pilot. He reached into the cockpit and handed his pilot's license to her.

Kerry read over Yvette's shoulder. "I'm trying to figure out your age," said Yvette. "You're twenty-nine?"

He nodded.

"Can I smell your breath?"

He wiped his mouth with the back of his hand and gave her a deep back-of-the-throat huff.

"You smell like Colgate."

"I don't drink on the job, if that's what you're looking for. In fact, I don't drink at all."

Yvette was chewing hard on her lip, as if she might bite right through it. "Do you have a maintenance log?"

The pilot fished out a book from the back of his seat. "Had her in last week. She purrs like a cougar."

Yvette closed the log. "Okay," she sighed. "I'm in."

Kerry high-fived Yvette as she buckled her into the plane. "Hey, you forgot something, doofus—like your gear!" She hurried back to retrieve Yvette's pack from the truck, before Yvette could change her mind.

Harcourt oozed in beside the pilot, while Yvette sat behind Matthew and Kerry behind Harcourt. "If you need me during the flight, Yvette, kick my chair," said Matthew. "And call me Matt."

Kerry watched Yvette sit back in her seat, arms rigid. She leaned over and patted her forearm, saying, "It's going to be okay." She knew she didn't sound convincing.

"Keep your hard hat on your lap. It makes a decent barf bag. I mean, after that party last night, anything can happen," Yvette said.

"Like you had to remind me." Kerry winced, feeling as though she could barf—from nerves, not alcohol. While she was relieved that Yvette seemed better, she worried that the pontoons of this overloaded plane were digging their heels into the water.

Before takeoff, Matthew checked the girls' seatbelts. He had low words of encouragement for Yvette as the motor warmed up, before the plane taxied from the dock. The smell of fuel, heavy and sweet, caught Kerry's nose as the plane plowed the water at a steady speed. This felt like the beginning of a dance competition, before the music started. Her body was tingling with anticipation, her mind clear, her stomach doing flip-flops, when, about two hundred yards from shore, the plane stopped and turned into the wind. She held her breath as the engine accelerated and whined more and more loudly, the plane going faster and faster. *You can do this, honey,* she heard her father say. While her mother bossed and nagged her, her father had faith in her. *You can do this.* She willed the plane to lift off the water and begin to climb. When it was finally high in the air, she wanted to clap with the joy of it. This must be how a mother robin felt when a baby bird, flopping and floundering on the ground, finally put it all together. Exhilarating!

Kerry looked down to see diamonds flashing on the water and tin roofs winking in the sun. As they climbed higher, the landscape resolved into a relief map, and she followed roads and watercourses from source to outlet, hundreds of lakes and rivers shimmering like mica. The green was intense against the blue but soft at the same time. She sensed that if she jumped out, she'd flutter through the air like a poplar leaf, twisting and turning and landing lightly in the arms of a giant pine.

The plane banked and straightened out, and she could see the black stripe of the highway below them. She lost track of time, mesmerized by the landscape below. Was that an old iron mine? There was a gravel pit, big enough to hold a fleet of trucks. A dump with the garbage neatly sorted. There was— The plane bounced and swayed while her stomach played catch-up. They dropped through the air and her hard hat rolled off her lap. Chalky white smoke swirled around the plane. A trickle of sweat ran down the inside of her arm.

Matt was flying blind.

Kerry looked at Yvette. She was whimpering, with her eyes shut tight. Kerry reached over and touched her hand but Yvette paid no attention, continuing to white-knuckle the armrests.

The plane shuddered and rattled until Kerry thought her head would blow off. She hugged her legs to her chest, as tightly as she could and still keep her seatbelt on. She held her breath and felt sweat rolling down her face. Finally the plane breasted the smoke and steadied. Brilliant blue sky stung her eyes as Matthew skirted the edge of the fire on the windward side.

Where to look! It wasn't one continuous wall of fire, like Kerry had imagined. Her eyes popped from one patch of flames to another, as far as the horizon. Full-grown trees exploded into fire, bursts of flame rose two and a half times the height of the trees. Black smoke swirled and eddied, then turned muddy brown. Flames—yellow, orange, red—blotted out the forest floor as the fire raced up one tree after another, then leaped, tree to tree, across the forest canopy. Kerry imagined the underside of the plane below her blistering in the savage heat.

She spotted a tiny orange helicopter lower down, with a bucket the size of a thimble swaying under it, dropping a spray of water that vaporized before it even hit the trees. The scale of that little machine, against a vast bank of oily black clouds, made the exercise of firefighting seem hopeless. The fire was like a pack of wild beasts surging here and there across the landscape, racing, pausing, shape-shifting, as it searched for more oxygen to gobble up. Her heart pounded as she scanned the ground to see if she could spot the firefighters. Was Aubrey down there?

As the plane dropped lower and lower, looping in circles, Kerry spied a scraggle of canvas tents on the verge of a lake. Matthew did a couple of practice flybys to inspect the lake and she could see the shift from light to dark where the water got deeper. She sensed that he was ready to land when he came in low over the tree-tops, and squeezed her eyes tight. The plane dropped hard and fast. *The sky is falling. The sky is falling.*

The pontoons touched the water, skimming its surface, and the tail bobbed up as it taxied to a raft anchored just off the campsite. Harcourt, his bald head glistening with sweat, flung open the door and gulped in big breaths. Matthew yelled at him for opening it too soon, and Kerry thought he deserved being told off after the grief he'd given them.

"A piece of pie." There was a quaver in Yvette's voice, and her hands were shaking so badly that she had to tuck them under her thighs. *Cake*—but Kerry let it go.

"Yvette, look out the window," she cried. "It must be a sign we'll be okay." The girls unbuckled their seatbelts and scrambled for the door as Didier rowed to meet them.

"That's *our* boat!" Yvette said. "That piece of junk is following us everywhere."

"Watch it, girls," said Didier. "This thing handles like a pig." Kerry and Yvette smirked, remembering their conversation with their boss. "I'll take you girls first and come back for another load."

"No, you won't," announced Harcourt. "I'm supervising and I'm going first."

Yvette licked her finger and tested the wind direction as a froth of foam collected along the shoreline. Kerry noticed that Matthew looked worried and wasn't moving to help them unload. "I think we should get back in this plane and get out of here," said Yvette. "The wind has drifted."

Harcourt tipped the brim of his hard hat off his face, crossed his arms over his chest, and glared at her. "What the hell do you know from nothin', huh?"

"She's right. The wind has changed." Matthew jumped back into the pilot's seat and picked up a squawking radio. Kerry couldn't hear the words, but he seemed to be arguing with the person on the other end, and then with someone more senior. When he came out on the pontoon again, he removed his sunglasses and looked at each girl closely. "I have orders to leave you here in the capable hands of Mr. Harcourt. I'm sure you'll be fine."

"Are you saying you *hope* we'll be fine, Matt, or you're *certain* we'll be fine?" Yvette asked.

Kerry twisted her bandanna into a rope. "I'm not comfortable knowing the fire's so close."

"Well, you don't have a choice, so quit bellyaching," Harcourt snapped. "The road should be cleared pretty soon, so we can get out that way if we have to. Now *move*."

They set up a human chain and unloaded the plane onto the raft. Didier shifted the weight in the boat to make sure it was balanced, directed everyone to their seats, then pulled away as another boat came in for the rest of the cargo. The girls waved as Matthew took off and buzzed low before heading over the ridge.

Harcourt was first out of the boat and he was as rude as usual. "I don't want you girls getting in the way."

"Then why did he bring us?" Yvette whispered to Kerry.

"When you get that stuff unloaded, you'd better start on dinner. You can count on fifty guys, maybe sixty. And it better be good."

Didier grinned. "No pressure though, girls. I'll help you set up. Apparently I've been promoted to fire admin."

It took about an hour to lug the pots and pans, cooking utensils, and cases of canned goods up to the cook tent. "Sick," said Kerry, as she inspected the dirty white canvas thrown over newly cut sapling poles. "I can stand up in here. How come the canvas floor piece goes up the wall like that?"

"So we don't get our sleeping bags wet when it pours rain," Yvette said.

"This tent is just for cooking, right? We're not sleeping here?" said Kerry. "With the smell of food? I read on the Internet that it's not safe because it attracts bears."

Yvette laughed. "I don't think a bear is going to bother with us when it has a fire to run away from. Sixty people are going to be living in this camp, and men will be coming and going all night long. Bears are not stupid. Besides, you really don't get a vote."

Didier shouldered his way through the door of the tent and dropped his final load, two new Coleman stoves. "What's for supper?"

Without even checking, Yvette said, "Beans."

"Homemade, just like my mom makes?"

"Get real." Yvette turned to Kerry. "They always send beans, canned tomatoes, and Spam. You can count on it. Oh yeah, there'll be fruit salad so these guys don't get scurvy. Didier, we need some tables set up."

"And how are those bathrooms coming along? We

can't just unzip it like you guys." Kerry laughed nervously. She had been wondering about bathrooms since those scary moments on the plane.

"Whoa," said Didier. "Be careful about—you know, talking like that—around here. You may get more than you bargained for. These are tough guys. They take their fun where they find it."

Yvette nodded. "You think that fire over the ridge is dangerous? It's nothing compared to the danger to us girls in this camp. I've lived in construction camps all my life, at least until they sent me to boarding school. This is new to you, I know, but there's a code of behavior. The minute the men think you're loose, you've had it. As far as they're concerned, you're asking for it and you'll get what you deserve. Act like a nun and you won't borrow trouble. I can joke around a bit more because I'm older and I know how to talk to them, but you and I have to go everywhere together, stuck like Krazy Glue."

Kerry covered her ears. "You're freaking me out!"

"There's nothing to worry about if you watch how you act. Stick with me."

Together, the girls sat cross-legged on the floor and assembled the stoves. They carried them outside to fill up the tanks, and Kerry held the funnel while Yvette poured in the naphtha fuel. Then Yvette demonstrated how to pump the gas and light the burner, while Kerry copied her actions on her own stove each step of the way. "This is fun," Kerry said, when they'd finished.

"Fun? We can talk about that later, when you have a headache from breathing too many gas fumes. I hope we don't have to cook on the ground; my back won't take it. Turn your stove off now that we know it works." Yvette rummaged for stainless steel pots and big stir spoons. When she discovered a package of paper plates and plastic forks, she hugged them to her chest. "This will make our life so much easier."

Kerry hesitated before asking, "Is it really that dangerous? I mean, I know the fire is, but most of the men seem pretty nice."

"Just remember what I said. And don't think about things you can't change. We'll make the best of it, okay?"

"I guess." Kerry turned away and rummaged through a box where she found a cutting board and some carving knives. Yvette pulled out a tray of bread followed by several pounds of butter and cartons of milk. With each discovery, Yvette revised and expanded the menu, until it was settled that they would serve the meat buffet style and let the men make their own sandwiches.

By four o'clock, they were chopping a five-pound bag of onions and crying. "So, what do you think of Matt?" Yvette asked, tears streaming down her face.

"The pilot? I liked him." Kerry wiped her eyes with the sleeve of her shirt.

"Me too. He has nice brown eyes."

"Yvette! He's way too old for you."

"He's under thirty."

"He won't look at you twice."

"We'll see."

"You're crazy. . . . Okay, why aren't we just heating up the beans and dishing them out? Why are we adding all this stuff?"

"Because we only have one time to make a good impression."

"What if they hate this goop?"

"Come on, they're starving. As long as we don't burn it, it will taste gourmet. It's my papa's recipe, and we never had a complaint."

Yvette heated oil in the bottom of the pots, throwing four handfuls of onion into each and sautéing them till they were golden brown. She dumped in one drained can of tomatoes for each five cans of baked beans, and added two tablespoons of mustard and a half-bottle of Worcestershire sauce to the mixture. Meanwhile, Kerry was dicing Spam into cubes the size of the tip of her baby finger.

"See, it's a complete meal, *un pot-au-feu*. They'll be happy with this and buttered bread and sandwiches." Still, she fretted as mealtime approached. "Stir, stir. If there's one burned bit, the whole thing will be ruined."

"Stop it; they'll love it. I do, and I don't even like beans."

The men were arriving, their faces blackened with smoke. Some had tried to clean themselves up but they'd managed only to smear the black and gray around. They looked so tired that Kerry was sure they'd fall over if they weren't so tightly wedged one behind the other. She scanned the line for Aubrey while trying not to be obvious about it. Was he as cute as she remembered? She and Yvette moved forward to help spoon out the meal.

"You cookies have quite a little setup here," said Harcourt. He leaned on the table, checking it for sturdiness. "Hey, Didier, you did a pretty good job, considering."

Yes, Didier's our knight in shining armor, Kerry thought. As she leaned forward to serve the men in line, the smoke smell from their clothes caught in her throat and she coughed.

"Where's the ketchup?" Harcourt said. He balanced drinks and a bowl of fruit salad and headed to the radio tent. Meanwhile, Didier was buzzing about with a garbage bag, collecting used paper plates. A line formed for tea and dessert.

Kerry spotted Aubrey. He looked gorgeous in his orange jumpsuit, even with soot and dirt smeared all over. He looked more bright-eyed and alert than the others, who seemed exhausted. *Will he remember me? I'm a mess.* She removed the elastic from her hair, shook it out and made a higher ponytail, and then got busy opening mustard and mayo jars. She pretended not to see him, in case he wanted to avoid her, and *poof,* there he was in front of her.

"Hi," said Kerry.

"Hi yourself."

That's it? Either he hates me or he doesn't remember me. "Uh, thanks for the other night. I don't think I thanked you properly."

"No problem." He shuffled down the line, his long, straight ponytail swishing between his shoulder blades. He turned around and looked directly at her. "Did you make the drinks?"

Omigod, here it comes. She clasped her sweaty hands and nodded.

"They're good, but not as good as your dancing."

He remembered. Kerry's knees felt shaky. *Why do I feel so funny?*

"Hey, Skinny Minnie, no chocolate chip cookies?" Didier teased.

"Kerry's baking those tomorrow," said Aubrey.

"I am?"

The Lakehead guys laughed. "She's so gullible." Kerry felt her cheeks flaming. Aubrey noticed and offered to help her clean up.

"Pretty much done, thanks. These paper products aren't eco-friendly but they work."

"We generate too much garbage, a temptation for bear."

"But not here, right?"

Aubrey covered her hand with his and squeezed it. "Don't worry about bear when I'm around. Besides, the department is strict about taking all garbage to the dump."

He has a dimple in his right cheek when he smiles that kind of goes with his cleft chin. Why are they laughing at me?

All laughing ceased when Harcourt returned and began cracking his knuckles to get their attention. "The fire boss wants you to know that you're doing a terrific job under the circumstances, which I guess includes you two girls. The damn wind keeps shifting around but we're watching it. The fire is up to three hundred acres already and extra units are on the way from all over the Northwest. That's the bad news. The good news is that we've found evidence that the fire was started on the island in Trout Lake. It must have been a real hot one to jump over the water." He held up a baggie containing a bright pink Bic lighter and passed it around the circle.

Yvette's cheeks were as bright as the lighter's plastic shell. She passed the bag to Kerry like a hot potato.

When Harcourt had it back in his possession, he added, "We're sending it for testing at the forensic lab in Thunder Bay. If we catch the bastard who set this fire, he's going to pay for life."

Aubrey was watching Yvette closely, and he raised an eyebrow in Kerry's direction. She looked away quickly.

"Oh my God," she said later, when she and Yvette were alone in the tent putting pots and pans away. "It looks like yours."

"It *is* mine! I recognize the scratch under the flicker. I'm sure I had it at the party. Didn't you say I had my lighter at the party? And how could it have gotten on the island?"

"Honestly, I can't remember. None of this makes sense."

"Someone must have stolen it. Or I must have dropped it at the party and someone picked it up."

"But why?"

"Maybe to get me in trouble, you know, to make the evidence."

"Evidence of what? It's crazy. What should we do? Who should we tell?"

"Let me think." Yvette chewed the skin on her thumb. "We can't tell anyone. Harcourt would have me arrested. And you, too."

"Me? What did I do?"

"Nothing, but Harcourt would use any excuse to get rid of us. He hates us both. And I hate him, too!"

CHAPTER 7

"Where are my pants?" Kerry said first thing the next morning, as she rooted around in the bottom of her sleeping bag with her toes. She fished for her bra and underpants. "Who said last night that I'd stay warmer if I slept naked? Who was that idiot?"

"Me. Did you keep your socks on?" Yvette asked, yawning.

"Of course I kept my socks on, I'm not completely stupid. You look like I feel. You okay?"

Yvette squeezed her eyes shut. "I can't stop thinking about my lighter. Why is this happening to me? It's a nightmare; it makes me sick. And yes, you should have taken your socks off, that's why you were cold."

Kerry put her undies on back to front, considered leaving them that way, then started again.

"You look like you're making out with the entire football team under there!"

Kerry stuck her head out of the mummy bag and gulped some air. "It's cold." She did her bra up at the front and shifted the fastener around to the back, cringing at the icy touch of the underwires. Then she wriggled into her frigid hoodie and her jeans, stinking to high heaven of wood smoke. "Do I have to shake out my boots for snakes and spiders?" She pretended she was only joking, but tipped them over anyway when Yvette wasn't looking. "I need a shower."

"You could go for a swim."

"A polar bear dip, you mean." Kerry flipped up a corner of the tent. "No wonder we're cold; there's frost on the ground! How can that be? Doesn't the frost put the fire out?"

"Fire can survive winter in the ground, feeding on the oxygen around the tree roots and popping up in spring," Yvette said. "Trust me—somewhere out there, water is boiling."

"Well, it sure isn't in here." Kerry snuggled back into her sleeping bag and hugged Rover. "Wake me up when it's over." Yvette held a piece of white bread slathered with peanut butter under her nose. When Kerry sat up, she handed it to her and made another for herself.

"I'm sick of this crappy food. How come it doesn't bug you?" said Kerry.

"If you work at it"—Yvette crossed her eyes—"peanut butter tastes like avocado. We'd better get going. The guys will want coffee. After being out all night, that's all they care about. You could serve it topless and they probably wouldn't notice. Yeah, on you they for sure wouldn't notice."

"Very funny."

They went over to the cook tent, and Yvette gathered up some green garbage bags of canned food for the guys working in the field. As she went out the door she said,

"Boil the water, add the coffee, and when it's done, pour in cold water to sink the grounds. *Voilà*, coffee, and it better be good. See you later."

There wasn't a coffeepot and there was no town water. Kerry seized an enormous pail and went down to the shore, where water striders wended their way in and out of duckweed blooms. *This water is disgusting*, she thought. She hopped into the steel boat, rowed out about fifty feet, and peered deep into the green lake. She sank the pail with both hands and pulled it up quickly, trying to wash out the surface debris, but only managed to slosh water into the bottom of the boat while wrenching her back.

After hauling the water back to the cook tent, she pumped up the Coleman stove and lit the gas, filling the tent with the sickly sweet smell of naphtha. The water pail was so big it covered two burners, and she slapped on a flat lid that didn't quite fit. *How much coffee do I put in? How much water is in there?* She tried to imagine the pot filled with coffee cups stacked one on top of the other. There had to be at least forty-eight cups. She read the package instructions, then got out a tablespoon and tried to do the math. When the water finally hit a rolling boil, she found bits of grass and mosquito larvae rising to the surface, along with sprigs of duckweed and seed fluff. It looked like a witch's brew. Giving up on the math, she dumped in a full pound of coffee. Now the grounds were bubbling to the surface. *How long do I cook it?* she wondered. *Where's Yvette?*

The brew looked too pale, so Kerry dumped in another bag of coffee, and the tent began to smell yummy. She looked around for a strainer—how else to get rid of the grounds? Maybe the guys could strain the coffee through their teeth or their mustaches. *Yuck*. The coffee boiled and boiled, until the gas started to *psst, psst* and finally ran out.

I did it! She ladled out a scoop of muddy coffee and found it full of brown grains like sand. Yvette had said something about cold water. Kerry drizzled some cool water from the drinking bucket across the top of the pot, but the coffee was still murky.

"How's it going?" Yvette was back. She inhaled the steam from the coffee like some wheezy kid leaning over a vaporizer. "Smells good."

"No thanks to you," said Kerry.

"Now you have to shock it with cold water to settle the grounds." Yvette dumped half a bucket of water into the coffee.

"Won't it be cold now?"

"Not if it's done right." She dipped in a plastic mug, went outside, and held it up to the light, swirling the coffee, nosing it as if it were wine. She took a sip and swished it around her mouth, slurping in air and finally swallowing.

"It's okay?" Kerry was twisting a tea towel in her hands.

Yvette gave a little shudder. "Dahling, it's mahvelous. Let's hope the men are half Turkish, because it packs a wallop."

"Knock-knock. Are you decent?" Didier came in carrying a cooler, muscles bulging, damp hair tousled over his forehead.

Yvette poured another cup of coffee, added a tablespoon of sugar straight from the sack, and handed it to him. "Kerry's little pick-me-up to wake you up." He took a tentative sip.

"Mind the minnows," said Kerry. She checked the time on her phone, the only thing it was good for. It was only 5:35, and she already felt as if she'd worked a double shift.

Around two o'clock that same day, Kerry was buttering bread for sandwiches while Didier opened cans of pork and beans. "Didier, why are you here?"

"What kind of dumb-ass question is that? There's only one reason to be here. It's all about making as much overtime as you can."

"Harcourt says he's not paying us overtime."

"You're working on the fire now, so it's got nothing to do with him. Make sure you keep track of your hours."

"Is money the only reason?"

"What else?"

"Well, I thought maybe you liked doing something important, like saving the forest."

"You're so naive. Mostly it's not about saving the forest. Fire is a natural part of the ecosystem, and nature's way of regenerating certain species like jack pine. We're trying to save homes and timber, transmission lines, and whatever else is valuable. It's all about money. It always is."

"Sorry for being so dumb."

He shrugged. "You can smarten up, if you're open to it and don't act so superior."

"I act superior?" He nodded. "I don't mean to. It's just that I'm shy, and people don't get me."

He shrugged. "Sometimes you act like you're from Toronto—"

"I *am* from Toronto."

"Most of us don't like down-easterners. It was probably some useless down-easterner that started the fire."

"Help me out here. You're from Ontario too."

"We should be part of Manitoba. Northwestern Ontario is closer to Winnipeg than Toronto. All's I'm saying is, maybe you should mix more with the guys, and stop giving people those looks like they're stupid."

"I didn't realize. Thanks for the advice." *I think. He's so direct.*

"Anytime." Didier ruffled her hair as he went out. "Besides, you're cute. You remind me of my kid sister. I'm watching you."

Just great, she thought. *I'm like his kid sister and, worst of all, I'm from Toronto. Some things I just can't change.*

She could hear raised voices. As they got closer, she realized that Yvette was arguing with Harcourt.

"Yes you can go out in the boat and get fresh water. No you can't have a spare radio. There are none."

"If we ran into an emergency, at least a plane could come and check us out."

"I don't have time for this garbage. If you're refusing to work, you're outta here. Two less people for me to worry about."

Kerry peeked out the tent flap. Yvette was steamed and counting to ten. "Okay, we'll get the water but we won't go out of sight of the camp," she said in a calm voice.

"You'll go as far as you have to go to get fresh water. The last thing I need is an outbreak of beaver fever. There's a spring on the island northeast of here. You'll find it. And don't take all day about it."

Within an hour they were on the water, with Yvette at the tiller. "Move up," she ordered. "And put on your life jacket until we're away from the dock. Don't give Harcourt any more reason to be on our case." She gave it some gas and shouted over the roar, "Look over there at two o'clock." A great blue heron skimmed the waves and rose to land on top of a pine tree.

Kerry relaxed as the *wham wham* of the boat on the waves subsided. It was so green in the north, and the dazzle of light on blue water made her squint. Occasional stands of white birch looked like toothpicks standing in a jar. She trailed her hand in the water and the spray sparkled like diamonds.

"Hey!" Yvette shook water droplets off her sweatshirt. Kerry grinned.

Yvette checked the map on her lap, changed direction, and headed up the lake to the narrows. She cut the motor to almost nothing as a canyon of black rock soared above them, and the throb of the engine echoed eerily. Safely through the rocks, she opened up the throttle and cut across open water. *No one would ever find us out here if we ran into trouble,* thought Kerry. She shook her head, trying to get rid of such thoughts. *We must be nuts to be out here without any way to get help!*

Yvette was pointing to a white line along the shore. In ten minutes the line became a beach. In five more minutes Kerry realized that they were approaching an island standing in relief against the mainland. Yvette sped up more, the closer they got to land, and Kerry clutched the gunwale screaming, "Are you crazy? Slow down!"

Yvette laughed but cut the motor, and they glided over deadheads and shoals. "Grab an oar and push us away from the rocks," she shouted. She turned her attention to the motor, tipping it forward until the propeller was out of the water and leaving a trail of drips behind them as the bow v-ed smoothly into the sand.

"Perfect, if I say so myself. Hey you, you're supposed to compliment the captain."

"For crazy driving?" Kerry twisted forward in the bow seat, her back to Yvette, and searched the shore for wild animals.

"Get out and haul us up."

"I don't want to get my boots wet," Kerry said. It was a pathetic excuse, but she was embarrassed to admit how helpless and lost she felt, surrounded by wilderness. The place looked so lonely, so edge of the world, and who knew what was waiting behind that wall of green scrubby vegetation and dark forest?

"*Mon dieu,* get out of the damn boat before we drift. What are you scared of?"

Kerry cleared her throat. "What if there's a cougar or a bear? A bear . . . a bear might be hiding anywhere." She pointed right and left to rock outcroppings. Aubrey had said she didn't have to worry about bears when he was around—but he wasn't.

Yvette climbed out of the boat. She looked exasperated but she didn't make fun of Kerry. "Possible but unlikely. Do you see any garbage?"

Kerry shook her head.

"Bears can swim to this island, but unless there's food to draw them, they wouldn't waste their energy. There's lots of vegetation to eat at this time of year, and this beach is pretty barren. They would find better pickings elsewhere. But they have good noses, so I'll leave the lunch in the boat—it's not a good idea to carry food around if you don't have to. You have more to fear from blackflies than black bears."

They got the boat pulled securely up on the sand and looked around. There seemed to be a natural path extending away from the beach. Kerry kicked a couple of black clamshells with the toe of her boot, then turned around and looked back the way they'd come. The opposite shoreline was miles away, with nothing but open water and blue sky between. She automatically searched for a cell phone in her back pocket, and then remembered. *It's out of your control. Focus on finding the spring.*

She found Yvette in the center of a velvety glade, balancing on the crumbled foundation of an old cabin beside a gravel depression with clean water bubbling up from underground.

"Somebody liked this place. I think it'd make a good cottage lot," Kerry suggested.

"Except it's not high enough for a septic tank. We'd hit water before we dug down four feet," Yvette said. "Septic depth is usually a matter of elevation and distance from the water. Imagine a line to the surface of the lake and down. Sorry, I'm sounding like an engineer, but you get what I mean. Hey, did you make a fluff?" She made a rude *blurp*.

"Not me. But something really stinks around here."

Yvette struck off, following her nose, with Kerry lagging behind. "It could be an old outhouse but I doubt it," said Yvette. "More likely a dead animal, in which case it'll be disgusting."

"Please, let's go back," said Kerry, but Yvette ignored her. At the end of the path, close to the far side of the island, they found an old forty-five-gallon drum rusting in the sun.

"Something must be rotten in there," said Kerry, moving cautiously toward the drum.

Yvette put her arm out to stop her. "It's illegal to hunt bear in the spring," she said.

"Bears? Why are we talking about bears?"

"Someone put a dead animal in that barrel to lure a bear here. That's how bears are hunted, by baiting them. They're curious animals with powerful noses. They're usually vegetarians, but they won't pass up an easy meal."

So bears probably *were* around, after all! Kerry wanted to get far away from the barrel but she was mesmerized by its stinking contents. "That's disgusting. It doesn't seem fair to the bear."

"A bear can run thirty-five miles an hour so it's sporting enough. Besides, how else would you catch one? Hunting is very important up here because, as Papa always said, you can't eat trees. The tourist operators need hunting to stay in business, and there are too many nuisance bears breaking into people's homes. I've seen them rip bumpers off a car, trying to open the trunk." She looked around. "Over there, the path continues." She grabbed Kerry's hand and dragged her around the barrel to the other side of the island, to a felled and staked log jutting out into the water. Even Kerry could see it was a makeshift dock.

"I guess they boat over from that shore. It's not much of a ride with a heavy bear carcass, and the landing is sheltered from the wind."

"Do you think they've been here recently?" asked Kerry nervously.

"It's well used," Yvette pointed out. "Look how the alders along the shore have been bent back, and the wood looks green."

"It gives me the creeps."

"Me too. I've never seen anything like this. They must be poaching bear here—there's no other explanation."

"Do you think it's safe to take water from the spring?"

"I don't think we should admit we ever saw this illegal hunting camp. I'd rather go back to Harcourt empty-handed. Knowing him, he'd find some way to make it our fault. He doesn't need to know. We've never been here, okay?"

"I guess. What do I know?"

They hurried back toward the boat, and Kerry took a deep breath before she reached the putrid barrel, holding it long after she'd run past. She secured the bow of the boat for Yvette, and when they were settled, Yvette put the engine in neutral and pulled the cord. The motor caught.

"Kerry, it's time for you to learn how to actually drive, not just from a book. Don't look at me that way. It's not safe to have only one operator."

With much rocking and laughter from Yvette, Kerry gripped the gunwales and, crouching low, made her way to the tiller.

"Push that lever back to reverse. And don't forget to smile!"

Yvette kept giving instructions and Kerry did as she was told, and the boat lurched backward and then forward. Halfway across the lake, with the wind blowing in her face and the boat pounding the waves, she finally relaxed. Driving the boat was scary but fun. In fact, the whole day had been that way, alternately scary and exhilarating. They were almost back to the camp when Kerry slowed down to an idle. "If it's Buzz who's setting us up because he wants to get rid of us, I don't think we should come back without any water. He'll use that against us. Can't we just boil the lake water?"

"It would take a lot of fuel, but you're probably right. Maybe I can get Didier to order some and have it flown in. We will tell Buzz-Off we got lost and couldn't find his stupid island. He thinks we're useless anyway, so he'll believe that." Together they lowered the water jugs into the lake to fill them up. Then they changed places, the boat rocking madly as Kerry lost her balance and then caught herself. She watched carefully how Yvette docked the boat, knowing that next time it would be her turn.

Once safely on shore, Kerry looked back over the lake. A little puff of cloud hung over "Bear Island" in an otherwise clear blue sky. By the time they unloaded the boat, the cloud was gone and the island had melded into the trees. It was as if they'd never been there at all.

CHAPTER 8

Around nine o'clock next morning, Harcourt blustered into the cook tent. "Girls, we're moving out. Pack up all this stuff, pronto."

"Nobody told us," Yvette said.

He glared. "Didier got the call on the radio and it's on a need-to-know basis. Now you know. We're pulling out in half an hour. I'll send somebody to help you. Wouldn't want you to get a hernia."

"What's happening?" Kerry asked.

"A fireball is heading this way. Now move it!"

Kerry quelled the panic in her chest. "What's a fireball?" she asked, as Yvette raced around the tent, packing up everything.

"I've never seen one but I've heard stories. It's like a round, gassy ball of fire rolling through the tops of trees, going about thirty-five miles per hour."

"How far are we from the fire?"

"Oh, quite far." She sounded as if she might be lying.

"*How* far?"

"As the crow flies, about five miles. But . . . ah, there's a big lake between us and the fire."

Together they lifted cases of food and kitchen equipment to the overhang at the entrance. "Should we start taking this stuff down the hill?" Kerry asked.

"No, there's a chance the wind will change and they'll call it off. Somebody will be sent to get it."

They plunked down and watched the men run from one task to the next, piling gear in a staging area and rolling hoses. The scene looked like an anthill stirred with a stick.

"I feel useless," said Kerry. "I think we should help."

"Old Buzzy doesn't want us getting in the way. We have to be ready to be on the first truck out. *Maudite marde*, will you look at that!"

There was only one road out. Now it was blocked by a truck stuck broadside and buried up to its axles in sand. The driver gunned the motor and the wheels spun deeper. Harcourt flailed his arms like windmills, giving orders, doing nothing to keep the panic out of his voice, while the men watched, shifting from one foot to the other with anxiety.

"Dig. Dig! *Hey!*" Someone had hit Harcourt in the chest with a shovelful of gravel as he placed boards behind the back wheels to make a ramp.

"Now look who's in the way," said Yvette. "As if that's going to work."

The driver gunned the motor again and a sound like a gunshot rang through the camp as one board split, then another. "Damn," said Kerry. "He's made it worse."

The truck was hemmed in at either end by trees, and there was no way to attach a winch to pull it out. Could she smell the metallic odor of fear coming from the men's bodies, or was she imagining it? And where was Aubrey, and the other firefighters? Had they gotten out before the truck got stuck? Or were they working in the path of the fire?

"Imbeciles!" Yvette started walking down the hill. "Come on, you're with me, remember?" She strode toward the truck and spoke quietly with the driver, who was hanging out the window of the cab. Then she and Kerry stood well back. At the driver's direction, a kind of bucket brigade formed to the beach, only instead of water the men passed smooth, flat stones. The driver placed the stones like pavement under the tires. Kerry held her breath as the tires started to spin and an acrid smell of burning rubber filled the clearing. The truck swayed and lurched, then shot out of the hole. Cars, vans, and off-road vehicles flowed out the opening like water through a burst dam. The driver made a big show of doffing his cap to Yvette.

"Now Buzz is going to hate you for sure," said Kerry.

"He'll get over it. Let's ask our new best friend if we can hitch a ride." The driver warned the girls to be ready to pull out immediately. Men threw stuff in the truck higgledy-piggledy until he blasted his horn three times, signaling them to get aboard. Kerry and Yvette were first, and five guys tumbled in behind as the truck started rolling.

"Where are they taking us?" Yvette asked breathlessly.

"I'm sure they don't even know yet. Just away from here," said one of the guys.

Abandoned tents flapped like flags in the wind. Yvette nudged Kerry, pointing out their steel boat bucking at its anchor. Kerry gripped her arm as flames breasted the ridge. "Oh my God! What if the truck gets stuck again?"

"It won't."

"Yvette, where's Didier?" Kerry looked around at the men. "Did any of you guys see Didier?" They shrugged.

"Stop! Stop!" Yvette screamed. Kerry and the guys joined her. The driver stood on his brakes as Kerry flipped off the back and sprinted to Didier's tent, where the radio was still squawking.

"They nearly left you, come on!" She grabbed one piece of radio equipment, Didier another. With earphones and wires dangling, the two of them chased the truck as it slowly moved away from the camp.

"Sorry. Sorry," panted Didier. "I needed to make one more call."

A line of flame shot over the ridge and rolled toward the far shore. The power of the fire was spellbinding and terrifying at the same time.

"Such a waste," Didier said. "That fireball will suck out all the oxygen around the lake, suffocating everything in its path. And all because of careless campers. They'd better hope they don't get caught."

"Yeah," said one of the men, "the death penalty would be too good for them."

"That's for sure," said Didier.

Kerry gave Yvette a dirty look for lying to her about the fire danger. She watched as Yvette popped another piece of nicotine gum in her mouth and chomped so hard that she bit her tongue. Kerry passed her a tissue. "Serves you right for not telling me the truth. Don't do that again."

"I won't. Cross my heart . . . and hope to die."

Kerry winced. Dying was not something she wanted to think about right now.

PART 3

Base Camp Number Two

June 30–July 10

CHAPTER 9

"Welcome to Base Camp Two. Let's hope to hell we stay longer than at the first one!" the driver shouted. The men laughed and a few teased back.

Base Camp Two was a jumble of abandoned buildings with broken windows and sagging doors. Stiff from bouncing around in the back of the cab for the last two hours, Kerry could barely get out of the truck and staggered when her feet hit the ground. She faked great interest in the nearest cabin so no one would see the relief in her eyes.

Despite the neglect, this camp had an air of solidity about it. The guys were excited, pointing out features like a concrete garage that would make a fine heliport or a truck maintenance depot. Once screening was stapled over the windows, the mess hall would be bug-free. The camp was perched on a puddle of a pond but there was no well in sight. Kerry, who no longer trusted her first impressions, asked Yvette what she thought of the place.

"I like that they could pitch hundreds of tents if they need to."

"Hundreds? Oh my God, do you think the fire is going to get that big? Don't lie to me this time."

Yvette ran a hand through her hair. "Nobody knows. It depends on the weather. But don't worry, these guys know how to fight a fire. What freaks me out is that someone is trying to blame me for starting it. I didn't do anything. This is a nightmare."

Didier raced over to them. "I'm supposed to tell you that Buzz noticed that you helped get the truck out, which is all the thanks you're going to get out of him. He says your first priority is to get the radio set up in the mess hall. There's a storage room at one end that will make a perfect bedroom for you. Food's on the way. We're having steak tonight."

"That should be easy. It's a good thing my mother the bleachaholic can't see how filthy this place is," Kerry said, as she lugged the radio equipment into the building. "Didier, we need major supplies to clean up this kitchen." But Didier took off without another word. "So much for that. Is he crazy or what? He could have fried out there if I hadn't run back for him and he doesn't care."

"Those firefighters, they have blood like ice. Not me. Oh, Kerry, what about my lighter . . . ?"

"I don't know what's going on. But maybe you're right. Maybe somebody *is* trying to make it look like you're guilty."

"What am I going to do?"

"Well, you can't leave. Either you'd run smack into the fire, or you'd be arrested for not showing up for fire duty. I think you just have to keep quiet and see what you can learn. I mean what *we* can learn."

"Did you hear what that guy said about the death penalty? And Didier agreed."

"I'm rethinking Didier. He's not helping out, not getting us anything. And he owes us big-time," said Kerry.

"Owes *you!* You're the one who checked the radio tent."

"And you're the one who made the driver stop." Kerry linked her arm through Yvette's and they stamped up the wooden steps to the mess hall in their work boots. "Such a team!"

At four-thirty the next morning, a real-life professional cook stood in the center of the kitchen, appraising the deficiencies of the setup. Kerry and Yvette straightened to attention, which was hard to do without keeling over from exhaustion. So many more men had arrived last night from all over the province to eat rare steak, and the dishes never seemed to end. Kerry waited for the order for her to step forward and introduce herself but it didn't come.

Didier whispered in her ear, "Rolf's the top camp chef in the province, and they save him for the biggest fires. He has a reputation for being very tough but he cooks like a dream."

Rolf was an older guy, long and lean. His arms were gangly but made of steel, if the knots of muscles were any indication. He wore a crisp white crewneck sweater and a stretchy black pair of pants belted at the waist. On his feet were white steel-toed running shoes.

"The equipment is completely inadequate for the size of this fire. I'll need two full-size propane stoves with griddles by tomorrow morning." Rolf waited until Didier left the room before addressing Kerry and Yvette. "At ease, ladies. I can see this has been a struggle for you but at least you didn't poison anybody. Very sensible to be dosing the wash water with bleach." He rubbed his bald head as if he were drying it with a towel. "Holy ass-kissing monkeys, this kitchen needs an overhaul."

Kerry and Yvette sneaked a glance at each other out of the corners of their eyes. Was this guy for real? "We're very glad you're here, Rolf," Yvette said. "We tried our best but I was faking it. I'm no cook." She sat down hard on a kitchen stool.

Kerry hadn't realized how tense she'd been, and what a relief it would be to pass the responsibility over to Rolf. She was tired of planning meals with Yvette and trying to make something out of nothing. Yvette grinned at her, and Kerry wiped imaginary sweat off her brow and pumped the air.

The change of pace was breathtaking. Harcourt was in and out of the kitchen all day, taking away Rolf's lists and reporting back when he'd finished with them, only to get more requests. Kerry almost felt sorry for him.

Rolf handed Kerry a shopping list. "I want you to check this to see if I've forgotten anything. You know what's on hand better than I do. This is the meal plan for the next four days."

They were going to have meat three times a day, including roasts of beef and pork, whole chickens, and ham. And Kerry could only dream about what Rolf might do with coconut cream. She'd forgotten what real food tasted like.

"You're going to need a refrigerator for all this stuff," she said.

"I've requisitioned a refrigerated trailer and a generator, to keep the food cold but not frozen."

Meal preparation seemed almost incidental when Rolf carried the load. After their first dinner, several of the men came up to him and thanked him for such wonderful chili, with so many kinds of beans in the pot, and cheese toasts on the side. Had he added red wine to the sauce? And where'd he get the fixings for a salad? Kerry was so busy scrubbing and stacking shelves that she didn't think about the fire once.

After another supper—Mediterranean chicken and couscous—Aubrey, looking every bit the professional crew boss, approached Rolf in the kitchen. *Aubrey looks so good,* thought Kerry. *I didn't realize he was that tall.* The men shook hands for longer than necessary, and she got the impression that they might have hugged if they'd met in a less public place. Aubrey acknowledged Kerry and Yvette with a nod. Kerry turned back to the sink, trying to wash silverware with minimal clinking in order to eavesdrop. Her hands were shaking. *This is stupid, I'm going to cut myself.*

"Rolf, I know you're not fire management but you're connected. You could find out what's going on," Aubrey said. Rolf remained silent, listening. "The elders on the reserve have asked for my help. They are very concerned about the bear. They've gone crazy."

"I'd go crazy too, given the size of this fire."

"No, it's more than the fire. There've been a couple of random bear attacks about twenty-five miles from here, while band members were out fishing, and orphan cubs are wandering the bush, hungry and crying for their mothers. They've never seen it like this. It's bizarre."

Rolf was thoughtful. "Is it possible that some disease is affecting the adult bear?"

"We've found no sign of that, and no carcasses. It's as if the adults have up and vanished." Both men stood quietly, considering the problem.

"Aubrey, you can count on me to run a secure camp. I've already requested proper garbage bins with bear-proof locks. I could speak to the fire boss if you like, but right now I think a few bears are the least of his concerns. If I get an opportunity, do you want me to say something so the boss can reassure the band?"

"The band council on the reserve doesn't trust the authorities, so there's no point. But if you hear something useful, I'd appreciate it if you'd pass it on to me."

"With pleasure."

In the reflection of the window in front of her, Kerry saw Rolf and Aubrey shake hands again. Aubrey walked toward Kerry as if to speak to her, hesitated, and turned on his heel.

"Hey, chief, come and have a coffee with us and tell us about your dancin' girlfriend," someone called from the dining hall. As laughter exploded around him, Aubrey let the screen door slam.

No comment. No retaliation. But Kerry gave those idiots the finger, under her tea towel.

Aubrey was so handsome. So dark and controlled, kind of French but not really. Maybe he'd change his mind and come back to talk to her. Every two minutes or so, she flicked the hair out of her eyes and casually scanned the mess hall.

"What's wrong with your neck?" Rolf whispered in her ear. "Got it bad, don'tcha?"

"I don't know what you're talking about."

"Sure you don't."

And he wasn't the only one. Yvette hip-checked her, saying, "Don't go there, girlfriend. He's Metis and he's not your kind. I'm warning you."

Kerry felt her face turn red. "Get real," she hissed. "Besides, you're not my mother."

CHAPTER 10

Any time they got more than five minutes off, the girls stretched out on their cots to rest and read. Yvette found some moldy *Reader's Digests* that she could pick up and put down; she said they kept her from thinking about Matthew. Kerry pulled some paperback romance novels off the shelf—how disgusted her mother would be!—and found them surprisingly addictive.

When Kerry finally got into bed that night, she opened the current gem, featuring a stunning blonde nurse and a tall, dark doctor on the cover. She knew it was silly but she was too exhausted to sleep and her legs were throbbing. All that standing to wash dishes wasn't what her doctor had ordered. She knew she needed a good night's sleep, but when she shut her eyes all she could see were pine trees flaming like torches. She rolled over and rechecked the "door alarm" of boots and tin pie plates hanging from the doorknob. She hadn't forgotten Yvette's warning about how vulnerable they were.

She was still awake and checking her watch at four, and had barely nodded off when the birds woke her, well before Rolf's alarm went off. He liked to get the coffee started and then pound on their door at five, expecting to see their not so sunny faces within fifteen minutes. But this morning was different. *Whoa, it's smoky in here. Eerie. Kind of like dry fog.* She peered out the window. *I can't even see to the lake.* She thought about pinching Yvette awake but decided to let her sleep. She pulled on boots over bare feet and galumphed to the kitchen.

"You're up early. How'd you sleep?" Rolf looked calm. He'd lit Coleman lamps to penetrate the haze.

"Better since they hauled our trailer up here from town. I don't think I could have stood another night in the storage room, listening to mice and imagining them running over my sleeping bag."

"Sorry, kid, but you weren't imagining anything. Didier brought me a secret weapon." Rolf scooped up a tortoiseshell cat and plunked it in her arms.

"So cute!" She buried her nose in its fur. The cat wriggled and jumped to the floor. They watched as it licked a paw.

"And so effective. It left me five mousie presents this morning."

"Does it have a name?" Rolf shook his head. "What about Mouser? I mean, that's her job title." Kerry went to the stove and poured a mug of coffee, black with three teaspoons of brown sugar. "So should I be worried that we're being smoked out? It's eerie."

"It's business as usual unless they tell me otherwise, but I'll let you in on a secret. I'm always packed and ready to go. A fire this size is unpredictable, but hey, they know what they're doing. They haven't lost me yet, and I've been at this for over twenty years. It'll probably clear."

Shoot me! Twenty years of early mornings!

Six pounds of bacon were sizzling on the griddle. Toast was popping up in the toaster, and Rolf used a paintbrush to spread melted butter on the slices.

"Good coffee." Even though his back was to her, she could tell that he was beaming. It took so little to please him.

"How about a cheese omelet?" he suggested. "You need protein to keep you going. Mushrooms and peppers? Onion, garlic, and dill?" He didn't wait for an answer. With one hand he cracked six eggs, two at a time, into a bowl. He whisked the liquid until it was foamy. "For girls like you I use lots of butter. It's good for the skin and the metabolism. You're way too skinny. You need fats."

He popped two pieces of dark rye bread in the toaster and folded over the omelet, and white cheese oozed into the pan. He spread a big spatula of butter on the toast. He plucked two white china plates, his "secret stash," from the oven, and placed her plate in front of her, mounding wild strawberries between the toast and the omelet.

Rolf watched Kerry take her first bite. She closed her eyes and swayed a bit. "Sure beats the protein shake my mother sticks in front of me. With food like this, I could give up dancing. I wish you could cook for me all the time."

Rolf grabbed his fork and heaped omelet on top of his toast. "My wife might have something to say about that, but I'll go one better and teach *you* how to cook."

"Deal!"

"Big day today, with a management meeting in the mess hall. I'm going to have to give you girls a couple of hours off this afternoon. Don't get your girdle in a knot; I'll pay you for the time. Now go get that lazybones partner of yours out of bed. It's late. You can tell her that Harcourt has arranged for a big guy—six foot seven—to be a lifter and help you girls out in the kitchen. That should make her happy."

"Aye, aye, sir. Look who's here."

Yvette stumbled into the kitchen. She went straight for the coffee and the cardboard squares holding four dozen eggs. She always stood quietly by herself, cracking eggs into a flat frying pan, while Kerry, more the morning person, did whatever Rolf asked, from flipping pancakes to turning bacon to stirring porridge.

Yvette was fairly awake by six, when the men started arriving, and she helped Kerry serve the food while Rolf watched from his stove, already preparing dinner. Dishwashing was pretty much constant whenever there was a break in the lineup, and that took them to about ten. Rolf had a new trick he wanted to show them: he placed the silverware in a strainer, poured boiling water over it, scooped it up into a clean pillowcase, and shook it all around until the cutlery was perfectly dry and spot-free.

For the next hour and a half there was a relentless routine of table wiping, vegetable prep, and more dishwashing. Kerry's wrists hurt from all the chopping, and her nails stank of garlic and onion. By the time one meal ended, they were well into prep for the next one. Dinner hour was a chance to hang out with the firefighters, including the occasional female firefighter from another region waiting to take off for the bush. Then the girls did more dishes, swept the floor, and cleaned up, with half an hour's rest if everything went well. From three to five they did laundry and potato peeling, to be ready to serve supper from six to whenever the crews stopped coming, which could be anytime from eleven until three the next morning. The sweet spot in the day came when the firefighters lingered over coffee and dessert, and the girls washed more dishes, cleaned up, and prepped for the next day's breakfast.

With the big meeting happening today, Kerry was looking forward to free time from one-thirty to three. Her last job before crashing for the afternoon was to dump a pail of vegetable water down the hill. She hurled it without looking.

"Hey, watch what you're doing!" A really tall guy was standing there, naked to the waist, with shaving foam covering his face. He waved a straight razor in the air while groping for the towel on the table to wipe his eyes, found a basin of water instead, and poured it over his head. He rubbed himself down.

Omigod, look at those scars! Parallel cuts ran up the inside of each arm, from below his wrist to well above the elbow. From this distance they looked like strands of cooked white spaghetti lying on tanned skin.

The stranger stared at Kerry and she found she couldn't look away from him. It was like trying not to look at a car crash. "You can close your mouth," he said. "I don't bite, and no, I didn't hurt myself in an industrial accident."

"I'm sorry for staring. I mean, I'm sorry you got hurt."

"I don't cut anymore." He shrugged into a plaid shirt and left it unbuttoned, so that a dark, curly mat of hair stayed visible from neck to waist. *Man, he must spend half his day pumping iron to be ripped like that.*

"Come here." He beckoned her closer.

"Oh, I have to get back to the—"

"No, I want to introduce myself. I'm Slash, for obvious reasons." He held out his hand as if to shake hers. "Hey, do I act like I'm gonna hurt you?"

Even as Kerry stepped forward, she was aware that he was making her do something she didn't want to do, but she didn't want to offend him. He grabbed her two wrists in one hand when she came near enough and pulled her close. He rolled up one sleeve and took the index finger of her hand, tracing it across the cut on his wrist as she tried to pull away.

"It's just scar tissue that healed long ago. In some spots where the nerve endings are gone, I don't feel anything. Like there."

"Why?"

He dropped her hand. "I could bullshit you but I won't, because I'm a very direct guy. I went on a drinking binge for six months, two years ago, and slashed my arm for every woman I'd been with, till then, that is. I'm not up to date, if you take my meaning."

Kerry couldn't look at him. She picked up the pail and started running back up the hill.

"Lookin' forward to workin' with you in the kitchen," he called, but Kerry didn't respond. Yvette had to hear this. This was one scary dude that Harcourt had picked for them.

She was relieved when she rounded the trailer and spotted a familiar face. Matthew was sitting on the veranda. The last time she'd seen him had been when he'd dropped them at Base Camp One. Before she could call out to him, he pulled a long, skinny notebook from a pocket of his pants, flicked it open, and wrote furiously, his pen digging into the paper so hard that it looked as if he might rip right through it. *Such an intense guy,* she thought.

"Hey, Matt. What ya' doing?"

He looked as if he'd been caught doing something he shouldn't be doing. He shoved the notebook back in his pocket and his voice cracked when he spoke. "Nice to see you again, Kerry. Well, you caught me red-handed. I'm supposed to do my pilot's log every night when I book off but I'm way behind, so I have to be creative, if you know what I mean." He winked.

"Your secret's safe with me," said Kerry. "What are you doing here?"

"Waiting for the big meeting to start. I think they're going to make an announcement to do with the arsonist. Hey, have you seen the Bear Whisperer?"

"Aubrey? No, he's out fighting fires."

"Damn, I was hoping to catch him. Tell him I was looking for him, okay?"

Did this mean someone had figured out that the fire had been started with Yvette's lighter? Was Harcourt going to make a big show of having her arrested? Kerry's mind whirred as she decided not to say anything. What was the point in worrying Yvette when there was nothing they could do to change things? While her partner had a nap, Kerry lay awake, waiting for the police to storm past the door alarm and arrest Yvette. She did enough worrying for both of them.

Omigod, are those wolves howling? Kerry strained to hear a call that she'd only heard on TV. She pulled the blanket over her head and tried to make the noise go away.

Aubrey was waiting for Kerry outside her trailer when the girls got off at eleven-thirty that night.

"I've been trying for days to see you but it never works out. How about a little walk?" he said. "It's not smoky and the stars are incredible."

"Sounds good. . . ."

Yvette shone a flashlight in his direction and Kerry tried to imagine the scowl on her face. Aubrey was already walking down the path, as if he knew she'd follow him.

"You go on in, Yvette. I'll be okay."

"It's late," Yvette said. "This isn't a good idea. You're exhausted."

"Yes, Mom. I won't be long. You know I'm always too keyed up to go straight to sleep, and besides, I had a nap this afternoon." It was becoming easier and easier to lie.

Aubrey reached back a dry and calloused hand for Kerry's and guided her through the sleeping camp. When they reached the water, she sat cross-legged on the dock in front of him, her back against his knee because she didn't have the strength to sit up straight. His touch on her shoulders was like a whisper, barely there, stroking the aura around her. "You're a good person," he said, *"and* a good dancer."

"I feel alive when I dance. I love the intricacy of the steps, the pacing, the kicks timed perfectly with the music. The judges call me a 'pretty' dancer."

"That's good, isn't it?"

"Not really. It means I lack strength and confidence. At my level of competition, everyone is technically proficient. What separates the winners from the losers is the energy they bring on that day, where their head is at, really. I'm not much of a risk taker."

"Something for you to work on. Tired?"

"Wired. I can't fall asleep after a shift no matter how tired I am. I can't get the fire out of my head. Yvette collapses like a puppy but I don't. Whoa, those stars look close enough to touch."

Aubrey ruffled her hair and Kerry felt like a cat about to purr. He took her hand and carved an arc with it across the night sky, sketching out the Big Dipper, Orion's Belt, and the North Star. "And this constellation is the most important one to me, Ursa Major, the Great Bear. Do you see it?" Kerry retraced the shape.

"Good for you." He kissed the top of her head. "I want to talk to you."

"M-m-mmmm," said Kerry. "We're talking . . ."

"No, seriously."

She turned herself around to watch his face. Was this about Yvette's lighter?

"Do you believe in dreams?"

When she nodded, he continued. "I had a dream about a bear wearing a necklace of bear teeth dipped in blood, clawing at my window until I opened it. He told me that a hunter would pluck the eyes of the bear's ancestors and run away with them across the sea."

"What's it mean?"

Aubrey shrugged. "I haven't figured it out yet. It's some kind of premonition."

They sat in silence. Kerry was dying to ask him what happened at the meeting, but was afraid of the answer.

"Tomorrow there'll be an announcement that we're getting a new fire boss, and other new staff. Harcourt will be demoted, which should make him crankier than ever. I wanted to warn you because you'll still be reporting to him."

"Just great. Every day he's worse than the day before. Is a new fire boss a good thing?"

"He's from New Brunswick, which makes everybody nervous because he doesn't know how we do things. It's all very bizarre."

"What's bizarre is that Harcourt's assigned this weird dude, Slash, to do the heavy lifting in the kitchen."

"The excellent pay attracts all kinds, so be careful."

Kerry yawned and nodded at the same time.

"I'm not getting much sleep either, worrying about bad things happening," said Aubrey. He pulled her up into a standing position and put an arm around her waist to steady her. "I've been selfish keeping you out like this. It'll be morning soon, and we'll get to do it all over again."

He led her back to her trailer and hugged her to him. "Good night, dancing girl. Stay safe." He turned her around, pointed her toward the door, and waited until she was inside.

Kerry collapsed on her bed. Aubrey had kissed her head! He'd hugged her good night! She had to be dreaming. *Oh no, I forgot to tell him Matt wanted to talk to him. Never mind, now I have an excuse to go looking for him.*

She awoke hours later to rain plinking on the roof of the trailer and smoke wafting in from the open door, where Yvette was inhaling a cigarette as if she might turn it inside out. Kerry ran down the steps in her T-shirt and boxers, letting the water wash all the sweat and ash away. "It's fantastic. Come on out."

"You're so stupid."

"Because I want the fire to be over? I've had it with this place."

Yvette started to flick her butt out the door but ground it out on the railing instead. She sighed. "I have to draw you a picture of everything."

Kerry wiped wet hair out of her eyes. "Don't we want rain?"

"Look toward the horizon. The damn lightning strikes are starting more fires. We're never going to get out of here."

"Shit! I'm so stupid."

"In a lot of ways."

"Meaning?"

"Come on, you have to know. Your mother never warned you about mixing races?"

Kerry looked at her partner for a long time before answering. Maybe she'd misunderstood what Yvette was saying, like so many things up here that she didn't get. One part of her wanted to run away from this horrible question, and the other part wanted to high-kick Yvette into the lake. Finally she said, "I'm really hoping this has nothing to do with Aubrey."

Yvette squinted. "It's about *you and* Aubrey. You are crossing a line there."

"I can't believe you're saying this."

"This is a small bunch of people. Cut yourself off from the pack and you'll never get back in."

"I don't care," said Kerry defiantly, but she felt queasy.

"*I* care. Where you are, I am. What you do, I do just being your partner."

"Piss off! You're not me." Kerry stalked back into the bedroom and Yvette followed her.

"Piss off yourself. That guy, he's trouble, but you're too naive to see it."

"And you're racist!"

Yvette folded her arms. "You've got to be kidding."

"If you're not, why do you have a thing about Aubrey?"

"I have experience. I don't trust him. Why do you like him, anyway? Because you think he's cute? Or because you think it's romantic that he's Metis? Is that how it goes in those dumb books you keep reading?"

Kerry bristled. "I like him because I like him. I get to do that, you know. I get to decide who I like. Who do you think you are?"

Yvette blinked like an owl. Then she shrugged and said, "Okay, you go on, get yourself in the middle of a shit storm. Do what you want."

Kerry felt tears well up in her eyes. She turned and ran out into the rain and down the path to the girls' outhouse, slammed the door, and barred it shut. She sat in the dark listening to the rain on the metal roof. Her dance friends would never believe that she was sitting here alone in a stinky bathroom. But where else could she get away from always, always being with Yvette?

How dare she tell me who I can be friends with? She's probably jealous that Aubrey likes me. And she's been striking out with Matt. She can go screw herself. And this Krazy Glue stuck-together thing is over. I've got one mother who drives me mental and she's more than enough, thank you very much.

CHAPTER 11

Kerry couldn't tell one day from the next, especially now that she was talking to Yvette as little as possible. She was sure it was still July but beyond that she didn't have a clue. She was thirsty all the time, and although she drank gallons of boiled water, her thirst was never satisfied. There was always a vertical line of sweat between her breasts, although she kept pulling her cotton t-shirt away from her skin and flapping it up and down.

It was almost impossible for two girls to keep up with the dishes for three hundred men, even with the help of Slash and the other conscripts that Rolf managed to collar. Hour after hour they stood beside each other, washing and drying, washing and drying, rarely speaking. Besides, they'd run out of things to say.

This morning, Kerry's entire body seemed to be encased in liquid salt. She could taste herself on her upper lip. "Are you hot, Yvette?"

"Hot hot, and not in a good way."

Rolf's supply requisition was on the table. Kerry picked up a pencil and added, "Two cans of baby powder. One large jar of petroleum jelly. Ice." She swayed at the thought of smooth, soft baby powder sliding along damp flesh, between waistband and skin. She could conjure up the faint smell of it. Petroleum jelly could be slapped between thighs that rubbed together fourteen hours each day. It would also protect hands that spent too much time in water and bleach, and were beginning to crack along the knuckles in long, deep cuts that never healed.

Kerry added, "Gatorade and two pairs of white cotton gloves," though she didn't expect to get them. It would be so good to slip her jelly-slathered hands into gloves while she slept. *Dream on.* She pulled the neck of her shirt up over her nose like a bandit, to wipe away the droplets that sprinkled her upper lip.

"Oh ye of little faith," Rolf said the next day, when he came through with everything on the list, including ladies' gardening gloves and deep-conditioning hair treatment.

"When I get out of this hellhole, I'm going to make sure Mrs. Rolf knows what a great catch you are," Yvette said.

Rolf was blushing. "I'm not sure she'll want to hear that from you," said Kerry.

"All right, you old goat, I won't tell her. *Merci beaucoup.*" Yvette planted a big smacker on Rolf's grizzled beard. The girls skipped out the door to try the new stuff, any hard feelings forgotten for the moment.

In the early afternoon, Rolf asked Slash to carry a hundred-pound sack of potatoes outside for the girls to peel. "You girls need some vitamin D. You're looking peaked."

Slash hoisted the potatoes on his shoulder and dropped the sack with a thud beside the picnic table. He took a dagger sheathed in leather from inside his boot and sliced the burlap string. When he yanked it, smooth yellow potatoes tumbled to the ground. He picked one up and sniffed deeply, then tossed it to Kerry. "Catch! Nothing like the smell of potatoes fresh out of the ground. Earthy, you know what I mean?"

Kerry examined the potato. It was well washed, with only a few pesky eyes she'd have to gouge out with the peeler. The skin, thin and flaky, looked easy to peel.

Slash went back to the kitchen and returned with a scrub basin full of water. He set it down on the ground, midway along the bench seat of the table. "You two can practice your basketball shots."

"That'll be the day," said Yvette.

One by one, Slash picked up the paring knives spread on the table and tested them with his thumb, grimacing as if someone had insulted him. He pulled a stone from the back pocket of his jeans, dunked it in the potato water, and started to sharpen the blade of a knife.

"Rolf did that yesterday," said Kerry.

"Each day around here is like a regular week. Needs to be done again."

Talking about knives with Slash felt like talking about drinking around an alcoholic—awkward and dangerous. Kerry didn't know how to change the subject so she concentrated on peeling a potato.

"You get a worse cut with a dull knife than a sharp one," he said.

The sun glinted off the blade. Kerry shifted down the bench to protect her eyes.

"Me sharpening these knives, is that bothering you?"

"Speaking for myself, yes, you're bugging my ass!" said Yvette. "You can leave anytime."

"Could but won't. Old Rolf's taken a shine to me and this is a good job with lots of hours. If there's something I'm doing wrong, let me know and I'll try and fix it. No promises, though."

"Your presence bothers me." Yvette's eyes never left the scars exposed below the wristbands of his long-sleeved shirt. "Sorry, I missed your name."

"*Slash* will do. Thank you for being straight up. I like my women straight up."

Kerry traded her knife for the one that Slash just sharpened. If she kept her hands busy, she could listen to the two of them sniping at each other without participating.

"So refined of you, Monsieur Slash-and-Burn," said Yvette. "What gives with the cutting?"

Kerry felt her face flame. Now he knew she'd been talking about him behind his back.

"I explained that to your young friend, and that's all I have to say on the subject. I'm trusting it won't come up again." Slash tested the second paring knife with his thumb. "Now, this is a honey." He handed it to Yvette, handle first. "Careful, little lady. Don't do anything I wouldn't do." He swaggered up the steps carrying a tub of peeled potatoes, his skinny black form etched against the smoke reaching from the ground high into the blue, blue sky.

"He knows we're watching his skinny ass," said Yvette. "He reminds me of a water snake, so quiet and slippery."

Slash turned around. "Did you girls ever see the movie *The Bodyguard?*" They nodded. "I could be your Kevin

Costner. I mean, there's only two of you, and all those men out there. If you need protecting, I'm your man. I know how to handle myself. If you need me, just whistle."

Yvette burst out laughing. "You're kidding, a nut-bar like you?"

"Suit yourself." He carried the tub of potatoes into the kitchen.

"Don't let him get you going, Kerry," Yvette warned. "His knight-in-shining-armor routine is just a trick to get into your pants."

"Doubt it. He's always watching the men at dinner, making sure they don't come near us. He may look rough but he seems legit. Why do you always think the worst of people just because they're different?" Kerry stood up and walked around to the other side of the table, with her back to Yvette. They finished the hundred-pound sack of potatoes in silence.

When she finally got a break that afternoon, Kerry was slippery with sweat and the lake water looked cool and clean. She set the laundry basket on the dock. *Who needs a bathing suit?* She kicked off her work boots and did a shallow dive off the dock. The water was soft, like brown velvet, and she backstroked lazily to the center of the lake. She let her legs drop to test how deep it was and her toes touched some weeds. *I wonder if there are fish in this lake?* She swam to a gray stump sticking out of the water, gripped it, and, face down, blew bubbles and flutter-kicked. It felt good on her legs, better than physiotherapy.

I should do this every day! There are benefits to being here, that's for sure. It's so peaceful, so freeing to swim in water like this, under such a stunning blue sky. She imagined she was an otter and dove down three feet, opening her eyes and being dazzled by the shaft of sunlight reaching below the surface and disappearing under her body.

She hated to get out of the water, but there was laundry to do. Laughing like a little kid, she shook herself off and walked barefoot back to the trailer to change.

"The water is fantastic," she said to Matt as he came out of his room. "You should go for a swim."

"I don't think so." He took her arm and looked at her closely. Then he ordered her to go with him to the kitchen, where they found Slash and Yvette stacking plates. Slash doubled over, laughing.

"What's so funny?" Kerry asked, trying to straighten her hair.

"She doesn't have a clue, this one!" Slash wheezed.

Rolf was also trying hard not to laugh. He picked up the big kitchen saltshaker. "Close your eyes, Kerry, while I douse you with this."

"Salt? What for? What's the matter with you people?"

She felt Rolf sprinkling salt on her neck, then on her throat and behind her ear, and finally on her forehead. "Looking good," he said. She could feel him peeling something off her skin with a paper towel. "Shriveling up nicely."

"What's shriveling?" Kerry's eyes sprang open.

"Leeches."

"What are leeches?"

Rolf opened the paper towel up to show her five

disgusting black blobs. "Five big, fat bloodsuckers stuck like Band-Aids to that beautiful face of yours."

"Oh my God! Gross! Are they gone?"

"You're okay, Kerry," said Yvette. "But if they stay on long enough, they'll leave—"

"A love bite!" said Slash.

"What about the rest of me?" Kerry tried to look at the backs of her legs.

The others dropped to their haunches and had her turn around as they examined her bare skin, including between her toes. Rolf whistled and began picking at the skin on her legs. Yvette gently lifted Kerry's T-shirt and put it back down.

"Time to hit the showers, girlfriend."

"Stop laughing! What else is wrong?"

"Kerry, only you would put your hand in a nest of baby leeches. You're covered," Matt said.

"Ohhh! Get them off me! Get them off me!" Kerry was running on the spot and swiping at her legs with her hands.

"They're too small to hold on so they can't hurt you," Matt assured her. "Did you never wonder why no one swam in that lake?"

"Well, now she knows," said Rolf. "She learned the hard way. Take the salt, just in case."

"Don't laugh at me! This isn't funny!" Kerry said, trying not to cry.

"Rite of passage, darlin'," Slash told her. "We've all been there, more or less. You're just late to the party. You're gonna be fine."

Next morning, Rolf was standing in the middle of the kitchen staring into space. Smoke from the bacon was beginning to mingle with the fire smoke suspended in the air. Kerry grabbed a spatula and moved the bacon to the edges of the grill. "Earth to Rolf. What's the matter?"

"This here's a memo from the new fire boss saying he's decided to impose shifts in the camp, and you girls are now on separate shifts. Never heard of such a thing."

Kerry plunked down hard on a stool. "He can't do that!" She fanned her face with a dish towel.

"That new fire boss, he's really pissing me off. He's gone way too far," said Yvette. Kerry watched her tear out of the room, not hearing Rolf yell that he'd talk to him about it.

"I'd better go with her."

Mr. Sirois, the fire boss, was at his desk, writing in a journal, when Yvette startled him and his fountain pen streaked across the page.

"Now look what you've done." His face was red and blotchy. "And you too," he said to Kerry, who was trying to catch her breath.

"Sorry, sir. We're here about your decision to split us up. We can't be on separate shifts," Yvette said. The fire boss pursed his lips and she continued. "Monsieur, please. It's dangerous to split us up. In Ontario, students have the right to refuse to do dangerous work, and this would be very *dangereux*. Maybe you don't know this because you're from New Brunswick. We are just two girls with all these men. Also, there's more than enough work for two. One person can't do all the lifting and serving of three hundred big men. Please accept that our buddy system reduces the risks."

"Are you finished?" The fire boss took a deep breath. "You made your point," he said. "Okay, you can stay together. Now get the hell out of here. Both of you."

Kerry could almost hear his "Before I change my mind!" She grabbed Yvette's hand and tugged.

"*Merci, monsieur.*"

"Wait one minute, little girl. Are you the one who smokes?"

Kerry watched Yvette pale. "Not anymore, sir. I quit a long time ago."

He looked as if he was going to ask her more questions, but then motioned them to get out of his sight. They ran back to the kitchen to tell Rolf the good news and there were high fives all around. But Kerry's joy was tainted by the fire boss's question. Did he suspect that the lighter was Yvette's? Although she'd never say so to Yvette, Kerry was sure someone had put that idea in his head.

CHAPTER 12

When Kerry and Yvette arrived for work next morning, Rolf was waving a piece of paper. "What do the bloody arseholes in management expect me to do now? Turn water into wine?"

The girls read the fax: "Refrigerated trailer of beef departed Winnipeg food terminal 0400 hours. Truck intercepted en route by persons unknown. Reported missing."

"How can a whole truck go missing?" Kerry asked.

"It's more profitable to steal butchered beef than to rustle cattle," said Rolf. "Easier, too. I need you girls to get your butts to Dryden and do some major shopping for me."

Yvette clutched a damp tea towel to her chest. "Dryden?" she breathed.

"It's not Paris, Yvette. Here's my list. Be careful out there."

Kerry took the wheel of the van, and Yvette crawled into the back seat with her pillow. Before they got out of camp, Didier came running out and flagged them down. "Here's the fire boss's order too. Make sure you get

everything, even if you have to go all the way to Kenora,"
he panted. "The bastard watches every move I make, so
we can only hope the Scotch will chill him out. Oops, and
can you get some cat food for Mouser?" He smacked the
back of the van as Kerry pulled away. "Drive safely."

Traveling south on the highway was Kerry's first opportunity to see a burned-out area up close. Spontaneously,
tears streamed from her eyes, blurring her vision so that
she had to brake and grind to a stop on the gravel shoulder.
She put her head on the steering wheel and wept at the gray
landscape that surrounded her. So much had already been
lost, and this fire was not nearly over. Up and over the
ridge, and right down to the highway, the ground was deep
with ash as fine as talcum powder. Here and there the
charred remains of stumps, hollowed-out tubes, splintered
toward the sky. Up the hill, black tree trunks lay scattered
on the ground, as messy and useless as spent toothpicks.
In some places the fire had burned deep patches, tufted
around the edges with green trees. She could follow the
pattern of how the blaze had flared and skipped from hot
spot to hot spot, burning and moving on with breathtaking
randomness. A tract of forest was destroyed right to the
lakeshore, and the brooks that snaked through it were inky
black with soot and washed-out soil.

She got out of the car and stepped gingerly off the
shoulder, ash puffing around her ankles like moondust
around Neil Armstrong's boots. The acrid smell of wood-
smoke clawed at her nose and throat and she doubled
over, coughing. High up on the ridge, she could make
out orange, antlike figures looking for hot spots where
the fire might still be smoldering. Maybe she was

dreaming, but was that Aubrey waving at her? Just in case, she waved.

Back on the highway, she traveled at about fifty miles an hour toward Dryden, afraid that her misting eyes would send her off into a rock cut. Yvette was napping but woke up as they wheeled into the shopping center parking lot. "Oh God, I've missed shopping," she said.

"I don't think we're getting paid to shop for ourselves, ya goof," said Kerry. She stretched stiff legs and arched her back. "Besides, shopping for clothes seems—so meaningless these days. So trivial."

Rolf raised his eyebrows in a "you're late again" kind of look, but he seemed relieved that they'd arrived safely back at camp, though they'd missed supper. A colander of sliced strawberries dripped water onto the counter.

"I'm starving," said Yvette. "Sorry we're late but we got stopped by the cops. They were searching the cars but they let us go because we're with the department."

"That firebug's days are numbered," Rolf said.

Kerry grabbed a handful of strawberries and popped them one by one into her mouth, and changed the subject. "Rolf, did you ever work for Mr. Sirois before?"

"Nope. Why do you ask?" Rolf asked.

"His shopping list was kind of wacked."

Kerry and Yvette lugged eight bags of stuff to the fire boss's office, including hardware, toiletries, sugar tongs, plastic lunch bags, Maltesers, a CD of Shania Twain's greatest hits, and infrared night goggles.

"I gave it my best try, Monsieur Sirois," Yvette told him. "We got everything except the liquor. I had a bottle of Scotch almost paid for, but at the last second the little jerk of a clerk carded me and I didn't have my ID. Sorry, it was too late to go all the way to Kenora."

The fire boss folded his arms, his face getting redder and redder.

"See, Kerry's underage. We tried—"

"Trying doesn't cut it." He clenched his fist and Kerry thought he was going to strike Yvette. Instead, he turned his back on them and tripped over Mouser. "Bloody cat, out of my way," he said, kicking Mouser clear across the room, where the cat slammed against the wall and slid to the floor. It lay stunned for a moment, then bolted from the room. People had been watching, holding their collective breath, but now the clerks began reaching for papers and talking loudly, pretending they hadn't seen what had just happened.

"Hey, you can't do that!" Kerry was on her feet before she had time to think. "Am I the only one who saw that?"

"No harm done," said Harcourt. "It was an accident. The chief tripped over the stupid cat. And the cat's obviously okay." He held both hands palms up, waggling his fingers, inviting the rest of the staff to help him defend their new boss. When the phone rang, there was a mad rush to answer it.

"So that's it, then," said Kerry quietly.

"That's it," Didier chimed in. "Back to work."

"Didier, can I have a form to report an incident? I want to file a report about the cat." Kerry was aware that Yvette was rolling her eyes and shrugging her shoulders at anyone who would look her way, but it seemed that everyone was busy with urgent paperwork.

"That would be a form 2051," sneered Harcourt. "As in, maybe by 2051 head office will care about an accident with a cat."

"I want—"

"Missy, I don't care what you want," Sirois growled. He chewed on the end of an unlit cigar. "It's over. Get out of my sight."

Yvette jerked her head toward the door as Kerry dropped her eyes from the fire boss's face to the floor and retreated outside.

"Thanks for backing me up, bitch!" she snapped.

"Kerry . . . Kerry, you're so . . . damn . . . naive. I know this is your first job, but use some common sense. Sirois is no regular fire boss. He must have been sent here to find out how all these fires are starting. And he's in charge. He has the power to send you home and give you a terrible reference, so you'll never work in government again. If I were you, I'd find a way to suck up to that creep."

"Well, you're not me, okay? I don't believe in keeping quiet about that stuff. He could have killed Mouser, and he wanted to hit you. He's abusive. Maybe next time he'll kick *you* across the room. Am I supposed to keep quiet about that? Did you forget it's you he's after because of your dumb lighter? You make me puke."

Yvette reached for Kerry's hand but she threw her off.

"Leave me alone. You're as bad as the rest of them. Actually, you're worse. I hate you."

CHAPTER 13

"What part of 'I want to be alone' are you not getting?" Kerry continued skipping stones across the water as Yvette stomped toward her on the dock.

"I wasn't finished with you. 'Alone' is exactly how you need to leave this whole thing."

"I won't. He's such an asshole. I admit I overreacted, but I'm right."

"Grow up, Kerry." Yvette nudged her shoulder. "I'll let you in on a little secret. Sirois and his buddy Harcourt may be stupid and sexist but they have a lot of power. You don't see what I see. The fire boss hates you, and if he hates you, he hates me."

"It's all about you, isn't it? And what's he going to do? Fire us?"

"For starters. He could do that and then where'd you be? Serving coffee at Tim Hortons next year instead of doing kinesiology. Or he could send one of his buddies to rough us up. I think that was the point of his little display back there."

Kerry wrapped her arms around herself and hugged herself. "Seriously, you think he's a thug? Okay, maybe I could lighten up a bit."

"A bit? A lot. He really scares me. Nobody knows anything about him. And you're right—if he can do that to a cat, what would he do to me if he thought I'd set these fires?"

"Okay, I'll try to play nicely." Kerry hurled the rest of the stones into the lake. "But maybe I'll get a fire-boss doll and stick pins in it."

The next day, Kerry threw herself into the chores as a way to put Sirois out of her mind. As she scrubbed the picnic table, with soapsuds and bleach flying everywhere—reflecting that she was becoming just like her mother—she drove a honking splinter under her fingernail. She yelped and shook her hand to stop the throbbing and ran to Yvette for help.

"Don't suck it! My mom says a human mouth is dirtier than a dog's mouth," she warned Yvette.

"Remember that next time Aubrey wants to play tonsil hockey with you."

"Nice talk." She tried to pull her hand away but Yvette held tight. Blood was pulsing at the tip of her finger. The piece of wood looked gray and deep and felt like it extended under the nail all the way to the cuticle.

"You need to go to Rolf. It's in really deep; it could get infected."

When Kerry banged on Rolf's door, it opened immediately. He pushed her into a plastic chair and positioned a desk lamp so he could check the damage. "I can't see anything," he complained.

"Put on your glasses!"

He sterilized tweezers and a probe like a darning needle. Then he picked Kerry's hand up and gently patted it dry, and she jerked her hand away.

"Ahh, it's an ouchy!" Rolf barely touched the skin where the splinter had gone in, but the tweezers felt like pliers jabbing into her finger. Was he ripping off the whole nail? Kerry clenched her teeth, studied the grain in the linoleum floor, and crossed and recrossed her legs, resting her forehead in her other hand.

"Got it!" Rolf set the bloody splinter on a towel. "When was your last tetanus shot?"

"Last year, I think."

"I'll believe you. Now, the disinfectant is going to sting but you're a big girl. The worst is over. Hmm—let's talk about something different to take your mind off what I'm doing. How are you and your friend Yvette getting along?"

Kerry talked more than she meant to, in the stress of the moment. She learned that Rolf didn't know about Yvette's dad being killed in a plane crash, or that the insurance company hadn't paid up yet and Yvette really needed all the overtime she could get or things would be very tight next year at school.

"Looks like she'll get her wish, unless they catch the firebug," said Rolf. "But how many people carry a pink lighter, eh? Now, keep that hand out of water and we'll see how it goes."

It had been on the tip of Kerry's tongue to pour her heart out about how much she hated it here, but his comment about the lighter stopped her. Did he suspect

Yvette? Had this conversation been a fishing trip for Rolf to get information out of her about her partner? *Nah, I'm becoming paranoid. Rolf's a sweetie.*

Next morning, Kerry was no good in the kitchen. She couldn't wash or dry the dishes with one arm, and when she tried chopping carrots they shot like bullets across the room. She caught Rolf watching her more than once and gave him the "gauze up" sign with her whole hand. She knew she was useless but it never occurred to her that he wouldn't cover for her.

He waited until Yvette went to fetch apples from the pantry. "I can't have you in my kitchen, Kerry, you're a liability. You'll hurt yourself or someone else."

Kerry was determined not to cry but she had to bite the inside of her cheek. She'd injured her hand working her guts out for Rolf, and she was shocked and hurt that he was going to fire her. She turned her back and made light conversation with the men who were lined up, faces dirty with sweat and grit, hands so embedded with ash that they looked barely washed despite scrubbing with soap and water. The reason she worked so hard was that this kitchen was the only bright spot in their day.

Rolf tapped her on the shoulder. "I wasn't finished. I've got another deal for you, and I had to fight for it. I know you aren't the kind to sit around and do nothing. When you're healed you can come back, I promise, and I'll be some glad to have you."

Kerry gazed at him, willing her eyes not to tear up.

"Fire Support needs someone to file maps, answer the phone, and let the guy in charge have a minute to input data. I told them you have lots of experience. I kind of BS'd a bit, and now they think you're God's gift to the fire service."

She laughed. "I used to help out at my mom's office. I know my way around a reception desk."

"I'll let you in. They're out for the rest of the day, flying and mapping."

The office must have been a bunkhouse in times past, with warped pine floors, and wavy windows at either end. It had a picture window overlooking Leech Lake and was large enough to hold three plywood tables on trestles, cartons filled with rolled-up maps, and one computer workstation.

"There's lots of natural light," said Rolf. "When we're not smoked out, that is. And the roof's good. If it rains, the maps and computers won't get wrecked."

"Well, they're definitely organized," Kerry noted. Binders were labeled and neatly cataloged. The floor had been swept clean.

"The work gets away from them. They'll appreciate the help."

There was a stereoscope, a sort of 3-D viewer, set up on one of the tables. Rolf stood quietly while she had a peek through the lenses at the photographs the men were working on. "Looks like a hunting camp."

"Zoning in on the fire starter, maybe. Listen, is your hand terribly sore?"

"Only if I think about it."

"I'll shut up and leave you to it."

Filing took Kerry six times as long as it should have, until she perfected the trick of keeping the file open with her elbow. She date-sorted some memos sitting on a desk and couldn't help but see one with the word "Confidential" stamped diagonally across the front page. She turned the stack of papers upside down on the desk but she couldn't resist peeking. The subject was "No-Fly Zone."

She read the whole thing from top to bottom, including the attached map with hash marks showing the no-fly zone. There was an entire paragraph on what would happen if anyone entered the area by land, water, or air— dismissal with cause, no ifs, ands, or buts. The letter was signed by the fire boss and copied to Harcourt, to Matthew as the pilots' representative, to Didier, and to the minister of the Department of Forestry and Parks and a bunch of names she didn't recognize. It was as if the whole area had been cordoned off with police tape. But why?

Kerry found a clean copy of the map and marked the no-fly zone on it, then buttoned it into the pocket of her flannel shirt. She was careful to scatter the original paperwork back the way she had found it, with the memo buried in the middle of the pile. When Rolf showed up to lock the door, she was sitting at the desk with her feet up, flipping through a book on native trees of Ontario.

"It's dumb to lock it anyway," Rolf said as they left. "If somebody really wanted in, they could get in, no problem."

"Then why bother with the lock? Nothing else around this place is secured."

"By order of the fire boss, Kerry. Very specific instructions to me. Don't ask because I haven't got a clue."

Kerry opened the driver's door of Slash's crew cab and stepped up into the seat. It was the day after she'd started working in the mapping office, and Rolf had found her a supplementary job—driving Slash around the base camp while he delivered bottled water to the firefighters. She idled while he maneuvered a dolly from tent to tent, dropping off three cases of water at each location. She pulled the door closed with her good hand and it thudded shut, entombing her in forest green leatherette. An open bottle of Coke was sweating in the cup holder. She opened the glove compartment, looking for tissues or a paper towel, and a passport-sized document dropped out. She had no intention of snooping, but it fell open. She glanced out the window but Slash was nowhere in sight, so she skimmed the tiny print under a recent picture of him. *He's a commercial pilot? What's he doing wasting his time in the kitchen?* Something else was tucked into the document. *A motorcycle license? Now, that I can believe. But who is this guy, anyway?*

CHAPTER 14

After lunch the next day, Slash shouldered a sack of potatoes onto the ground near the picnic table. "Where's your friend, Kerry?"

"Beats me. Looks like I'm doing potatoes all afternoon by myself." Rolf must have been desperate to let her come back to work in the kitchen. Apparently Matt had been hanging around like a bad smell ever since Kerry had hurt her hand, and Rolf didn't like it.

She dunked a potato in water and concentrated on peeling one long, continuous strand.

"Hi."

"Omigod, Aubrey, you made me jump. How long have you been watching me?"

"I like watching you. I just got here." He took a paring knife off the table, tested it with his thumb, and got to work.

"You don't have to help me." Kerry knew she was blushing.

"But I want to. One of the helicopters is out of commission and I'm waiting for a ride. Might as well make myself useful. We got five new fires overnight."

Kerry felt her stomach tense. She didn't dare ask how close the fires were. She waved him off as if to say, *I don't want to know.*

By the time Kerry was on her third potato, the silence was growing awkward. "How's the bear situation?"

"Not good. They found five orphaned cubs roaming the rez. The elders set up a shift system to feed them, which makes the conservation officer happy, because those cubs are hungry all the time."

"What will happen to them?"

"They'll probably be flown to a zoo in Toronto or somewhere. Not much of a life, but they'll soon be too acclimated to humans to survive on their own."

"I bet they're cute."

"More than cute. I feel so useless, not being able to figure out what's happening to the adult bear. Some bear whisperer I am." There was a foamy scum on the potato water. He scooped it up with cupped hands and blew it into the wind.

"I always see you with your nose in a book," said Kerry. "Are you looking for answers there?"

"No, not that. I'm doing a distance learning program from the University of Saskatchewan in zoology and literature. Poets like Neruda, in Spanish—he was Chilean. Classics like Sappho. I find it interesting that three thousand years of history and culture have come down to us on paper, from long before electric lights were even thought of. A band member friend of mine and I decided to interview and tape as many of the elders on the reserve as we can. They considered me to be an outsider at first, but they're used to me now."

"And you speak Spanish too? I'm impressed."

"I probably should be doing something more relevant but it makes a nice change. No big deal. Hey, do you like fishing?"

"I went fishing once at a trout pond. It was fun," Kerry said.

"That's not fishing! It's a long way to my favorite spot in the bush. When this is over, I'll take you, if you like."

"How far?"

"Three days." He held her eyes.

Kerry thought she felt the ground trembling. Something was changing, that was for sure. She fumbled with the button on her pocket and pulled out the map in her pocket. "Show me on the map."

He studied the map. "This looks classified. Where'd you get it?"

She didn't answer. "Is your fishing spot on here?"

"Yep. Right here in this red zone, about five hundred yards from the dump. There's an old cabin I use. Shhh, don't tell anyone. It doesn't have a land-use permit."

She shrugged. "Who am I going to tell?"

"Kerry, I want you to promise me something. No matter what happens down the road, believe in me. Give me the benefit of the doubt. Promise you will and cross your heart."

She laughed and crossed her heart. "I don't get it, but sure."

"I'd better go now. But the truth is, I wasn't just stopping by. I've been avoiding getting to the point. Something happened, but Yvette's all right."

"Something happened to Yvette?"

"Yes—well, no, she's fine. She'll be back here tonight. She was flying with Matthew and there was nearly a collision in the air. Management is trying to keep it quiet, but I heard it on the radio. They don't know where the other plane came from."

"Could it have been one of those TV planes? Covering the fire?"

"I doubt it. The plane wasn't marked. Anyway, I wanted you to hear about it from me."

"Poor Yvette! I feel bad. We haven't been talking much lately."

"She's pretty shaken up. As a pilot, Matthew has some influence. He can probably look out for her. My concern is for you. There are crazy things going on; things I don't understand. Please, be careful who you trust." He grabbed her hand and pulled her up. "I'll talk to Rolf. You shouldn't be out here by yourself."

Kerry followed him into the kitchen. Maybe she should take Slash up on his offer to be her bodyguard.

CHAPTER 15

Later that day, Rolf kept Kerry busy doing food prep and serving. The men asked her where Yvette was, speculating that she hadn't been able to cut it. Kerry knew they were just teasing—they would be very upset when they found out what had happened—but it wasn't her place to tell them.

"Puts things in perspective, it does," said Rolf.

About eleven, after the dishes were done, Rolf walked Kerry back to her trailer, and together they waited for Yvette. With his awkwardness, Rolf seemed to take up all the space in the bedroom. Kerry ordered him to sit on her bed while she fussed around on Yvette's side, turning down the covers, getting out a clean set of pajamas and a washcloth.

"Do you think she'll want a shower?"

"She'll be dopey. I expect they've given her sedatives or something at the hospital."

"The *hospital?*"

"She came unhinged. Hey, *I'd* come unhinged if somebody tried to mow me down in a plane."

"Omigod. I feel like such a *biatch.*"

He passed her a water bottle. "I've been wanting to talk to you. What gives between you and Yvette?"

"Nothing."

"Nothing, my ass. And don't tell me it's none of my business. I got two girls here, and if my team isn't pulling in the same direction I'm screwed. I can't have the two of you fighting."

"We're not fighting. We're just not speaking. Much."

"What's it all about? You can tell your Uncle Rolf."

Kerry sighed. "Yvette has to be right all the time. She has to control everything. She's so bossy and it's driving me nuts."

"And what are you doing to bug her?"

"Nothing." He snorted. "Okay, she's pissed because I'm more open-minded about certain stuff. Also, I'm a very private person, or used to be, until I landed in this fishbowl. I don't think I should have to answer to her about everything. She's not my mother. And she's not my boss."

Rolf took a long pull on his water bottle. "So it has to do with some guy."

"How'd you know?"

"Eyes and spies, I have them both." He patted a spot for her to sit down beside him. "What I have to say is for your own good. Maybe this isn't the right time, on top of everything else, but here goes. Every day, at least five times a day, men ask me how much you and Yvette cost. What's your fee."

"For what? You don't mean . . ."

He sighed. "They want to know how much I charge for . . . a roll in the hay with you. They want to know my cut."

Kerry couldn't keep from laughing.

"There's nothing funny about it. These firefighters aren't Boy Scouts, eh? These guys look like professional firefighters in their orange jumpsuits, but many of them aren't the real thing. They're from all over hell's half-acre. They could be on probation. They could be hitch-hikers conscripted from the side of the road. They could be sex fiends, for all we know. They—" He held his hand up. "Is that a truck?"

Kerry levitated off the bed and yanked the door open. Yvette was holding onto the wooden railing, steadying herself for the climb. Kerry flew down to meet her, hugging Yvette's slight body to her. "Oh God, Yvette, I'm so glad you're all right."

Matthew stood quietly behind her. "I wanted to carry her in but she's bloody stubborn. She's loopy from the drugs, ranting in French. She's your problem now, Kerry. Come here, you," he added, to Yvette. He clasped his hands behind her back and hugged her. He stopped short of kissing her, but Kerry could tell he wanted to. Their relationship had moved to another level, she realized. Yvette had been right that she could make him fall for her.

"The doctor wanted to call her mom, but she's of age and she went nuts when they suggested it. Rolf, the doctor said she needs time off."

"Sure. We'll play everything by ear."

"Good night, girls." With one last worried glance at Yvette, the two men closed the door, leaving them alone.

"Do you want to talk about it?"

"I just wanna go to sleep." Yvette fumbled with the buttons on her shirt. Kerry helped her undress, with

Yvette being as docile as a toddler who'd fallen asleep on a car ride home.

Kerry lay in bed for what seemed like hours, listening to Yvette breathing and trying not to think of the alternative—Yvette not breathing. She was in that twilight before sleep when she heard a noise and saw an arm, attached to a shoulder and then a long-haired head, slip around the edge of the door. Kerry was instantly awake and her heart pounded so loudly that whoever it was had to hear it. She pulled her knees up to her chest under the covers, trying to keep her breathing steady.

How dare he! After all she and Yvette had been through! And what did he want? A shaft of moonlight projected onto the floor between the beds. He hesitated as if he was trying hard not to wake them. Whoever he was, if he came at her, she was going to propel him across the trailer and smash his head against the far wall. If he made one move on Yvette, God help him, because she was pumped.

Kerry shifted and the man froze. *Maybe now's the time I should scream my head off!* Then he cleared his throat and the sound rippled through her computer brain, looking for a match. He put one foot in front of the other, stopping when the floor creaked.

Kerry watched him open the top drawer of Yvette's dresser. There was a rustling sound, then a pause as he held something up toward the light and dropped it into his back pocket. *Dammit. The one night I don't pile on the door alarm.* He paused again, bent down ever so quietly, and opened the bottom drawer of Kerry's dresser. *What is he doing?* She felt a draft as he stepped back outside.

The trailer shifted slightly on its tires and the door clicked shut. He coughed and this time she recognized the sound. It was Aubrey! *Why the hell is Aubrey stealing from Yvette? Why was he going through our stuff? If he needs money, all he has to do is ask me for it.*

Kerry's stomach churned. Yvette had been right about Aubrey after all. She rolled over and smushed her face into her pillow, muffling her scream of rage and frustration. *I should have stopped him.*

Kerry managed some sleep, but in the early morning Aubrey's betrayal hit her in the heart. None of her things were missing. If she mentioned the theft to Yvette, on top of the near collision, it might send her overboard; if she confronted Aubrey, he'd deny it and that would be the last she'd ever see of him. One minute, that was all she wanted. The next, she was desperate to talk to him. *Why would he steal from Yvette? How could I be so wrong about him?* She knew that if she told Matt or Didier that Aubrey had been in their room, they'd involve the fire boss and blow the whole thing up into such a big deal that Aubrey might get arrested. Although Rolf seemed to like Aubrey, he was so overprotective of his girls that, more than likely, he'd slug Aubrey in the face and they'd both go to jail. And there was another problem. Every time the pink lighter was mentioned in Aubrey's presence, he stared Yvette down. If he was provoked by Mr. Sirois, he might accuse Yvette of starting the fire. *I'm between a rock and a hard place, as Rolf likes to say. I should tell Yvette all about it, but I won't.*

Kerry checked in at the kitchen before breakfast prep.

"Where are you going?" asked Rolf.

"For a walk." She brandished her cell phone. "You never know, I might get service. I'm a glass-half-full kind of person, stupid, I know."

"Stick to the highway, it's safer. And what are you thinking, wearing those short shorts? You look naked. And I don't like that tank top. Your boobs stick out."

"Really?"

"Nah, but your skinny little ass is hanging out of your shorts."

"Okay, Mom."

"If I was your mother, I'd tan your backside and chain you in your room. Speaking of your mom, here's a pile of letters from her. She must be writing you two a day."

"Thanks. Where's that bear spray?" When he turned his back to search for it, Kerry fired the letters into the garbage, covering them up so no one would find them. "Thanks. All right, you worrywart, I'll be back in an hour."

At the bottom of the stairs Kerry started to stretch, but she was too self-conscious about her butt sticking up in the air, facing the camp. She loped down the lane, and by the time she'd reached the paved road she'd made up her mind. *If Aubrey doesn't tell me what he's up to in the next forty-eight hours, I'll do something about it. I swear it. I don't have a choice.*

CHAPTER 16

"I can't believe it isn't here," said Yvette that evening.

"Did you say something?" Kerry was half in and half out of a romance novel, her fourth one this week, dumb but addictive. If Mom could only see her daughter, the ninety-percenter, now! There was something irresistible about the happy endings in these fairy tales for grown-ups. Who could argue with the appeal of a devilish rogue, a beautiful heroine, and everlasting love?

"My necklace, the one Papa gave me, is missing. It's the one with the arrowhead, Papa's good-luck charm from Newfoundland. It's Beothuk—that's an extinct native tribe—so it's very rare. I always put it in the same place in my top drawer."

Kerry was awake now. *Aubrey must have taken the arrowhead necklace with the bear tooth. It wasn't money he was after, but something sacred to native people. Because he wanted it? Or because he thought Yvette shouldn't have it?*

Yvette wrenched open the next drawer, and the next. "I took it off so I could get dressed up to go out with Matt, which was stupid, because if I'd been wearing the necklace maybe that airplane wouldn't have come right at us."

"Maybe." Kerry wasn't about to tell Yvette that her superstitions were silly.

Now Yvette was undoing every sock ball, searching each toe for her necklace. Then she started on her underwear. *"Maudite marde!"* she said. "Maman and I think that if Papa had been wearing his arrowhead, he wouldn't have died. He'd have taken more time before he agreed to go with that drunken *maudit fou* of a pilot." She pounded the wall so hard that Kerry thought she'd bash right through the fake paneling into the next room.

"It's not here," she moaned. "It's because the stupid door won't stay locked. I told Buzz-Off Harcourt something was going to happen."

"What are you going to do?"

"Report it to the fire boss. The thing should be in a museum." She kicked the dresser drawers closed and turned to face Kerry. "I think it was Aubrey. I know it was Aubrey." She ran a finger around her throat as if she were tugging on the leather thong. "Every time I wore it, he'd look at me like he wanted to rip it off my neck."

"You never told me this before."

"From the moment I met the guy, I didn't like him," said Yvette. "I don't trust him."

"Based on what?"

"My—what do you say, gut? First impressions matter with me, and I'm always right. When I think of Aubrey, I think, 'Fire starter. Thief. Drunken—'"

"Indian chief? Sounds like a skipping song, Yvette. You can't judge people so easily."

"Hah! You are not objective. Everyone can tell you have the hots for him."

Kerry pulled on her jacket. "I just have one question. What did you think of me when you first met me? Maybe you've changed your opinion somewhere along the line? Think about it." She closed the door quietly, not waiting for a response, and leaned against the trailer, eyes closed, heart pounding. *Aubrey, why'd you do it?*

Kerry went looking for him and caught him rolling hose.

"Hey you! 'From where does the thundercloud come with its black sacks of tears?' Neruda wrote that." Aubrey scanned the dusk sky, looking for evidence of rain. He didn't need to say that he wished it would pour—without lightning, of course. He'd already said as much.

"Aubrey," said Kerry, "I need to know something about a bad dream I had."

"Okay, I'll try to interpret."

"The other night, while I was asleep, I was visited by a large black shadow."

"Did it speak?"

"He had his back to me. I heard him sigh as if he bore the weight and misery of the generations that had come before him."

"Was it in the form of an animal?"

"A man. A man who unlocked doors and drawers."

Aubrey cleared his throat and avoided eye contact. She studied his face intently. "It felt so real, until a stranger arrived asking for help. A native person with an amulet around his neck on a leather thong, and he kept twisting and twisting and twisting until he was hanging from the ceiling of our trailer."

"Someone was fighting for his breath, his very destiny," said Aubrey. "Hanging between life and death."

"Really? Maybe my unconscious mind was just worried about Yvette losing her necklace. I have second sight, you know. From my Irish grandmother."

Aubrey squeezed her hand. "Let it go." He chucked her under the chin, trying to force her to look at him. "Kerry, you made me a promise. Trust me that there's an explanation."

She dropped her eyes and walked away, more confused than ever, and with no answers. *How can I trust you? I made up a crazy story that practically told you I saw the whole thing, and you still won't be straight with me.*

CHAPTER 17

Later that evening, Kerry charged up the steps of the trailer.

"Yvette, I didn't think you'd be in. How was your date with Matt?"

Yvette didn't look up from a dog-eared copy of *Vogue Paris*.

So it's going to be like this again, Kerry thought. *She must have seen me talking to Aubrey, and now I get the silent treatment. Well, two can play at that game.* She grabbed a towel and fresh underwear.

"I'm going to the sauna, want to come?" Predictably, there was no answer, but she could see that Yvette was dying to say, "Don't go alone." *I expected her to say something about Aubrey by now. She must really hate me.*

Kerry stopped by the kitchen. "Rolf, I'm hot and sweaty and my hair could get up and walk away by itself, it's that stinky. If I'm not back from the sauna in an hour, send in the cavalry."

The sauna was as dark as it was warm. She remembered to flip the sign on the door to indicate that it was occupied. She threw a saucepan of water on the stove and watched a cloud of steam sizzle toward the ceiling. She placed her towel over the wooden bench and sprawled naked on her back, her arm covering her eyes, yoga-breathing deeply in and out through her nose until she was aware of her breathing and her pulsing heart and nothing else.

"It's only me," Yvette called from the changing room. A cool draft accompanied her as she settled higher on the bench, closer to the ceiling, where it was hotter. "Warm enough for you?"

Kerry grunted in agreement. She dozed, then awoke with a start to acrid smoke irritating her nose and burning her eyes. "I've had enough. I'm going." She thought she heard Yvette mumble something. She placed a wet towel over her head and walked through the steam, arms out, like a sleepwalker. She felt along the doorframe, found the door to the dressing room, and shoved it open. The air was cooler here and she gulped fresh air into her lungs. How could Yvette stand it in there? She shimmied the towel up and down her back, over her butt, and down her legs. On the return trip, she looked up toward the ceiling.

"Oh, God!" The entire roof was in flames!

"Yvette! Fire! Fire!" Kerry screamed in her head, but no sounds came out of her mouth. For priceless seconds she was rooted to the floor, paralyzed. Then she hop-footed into her underwear and tugged on a flannel shirt, her mind going in slow motion. *I can't be naked with all those guys out there.* She grabbed a t-shirt and wrapped it around her mouth and nose. Coughing, bending low, she yanked open the door to the sauna and ran toward the benches. Yvette was lying on her back, a towel thrown over her face.

Kerry slapped her arm, her face. "Come on, Yvette. Wake up. Wake up!" But Yvette lay limp and unconscious.

She put her arms under Yvette's armpits and dragged her off the risers, bumping her body down the stairs like a sack of potatoes. She hauled her through the dressing room and dropped her at the outside door. She tugged the handle with both hands but she couldn't budge the door. Yvette must have wedged it shut to keep the guys out. Please, God, let me get it open. She tried to kick the wedge sideways with her bare foot, but only managed to shove it farther in.

"Help! Help!" She pounded on the door. She screamed and tugged and pounded with all her strength, until the door suddenly burst open. Cool air rushed in, and the flames flared brighter with the fresh oxygen.

Kerry staggered outside and fell to her knees as Slash muscled by her. He lifted Yvette's slumped body and started to run toward the first aid building, all the while yelling at staff to set up the fire pumps. Kerry stumbled after him, inhaling the night air and coughing. The smoke was so thick she could barely see, but she was aware of bodies hurtling by her. She looked back to see the sauna engulfed in flames, sparks spitting against the black sky. She heard the ping of shovels hitting rock, the rush of water from a hose, and the *chug, chug* of a pump. Mr. Sirois was silhouetted against the flames, shouting orders, his arms swinging, like a policeman directing traffic. The next thing she knew, someone scooped her up and threw her over his shoulder. *It's only Rolf.* She let her body and her mind go limp.

CHAPTER 18

Yvette coughed and gasped for air. "Kerry, turn off the stove; something's burning. Kerry?"

Kerry mopped Yvette's forehead with cool water. "I'm right here; everything's fine." She adjusted the crisp, cotton hospital sheet across Yvette's chest.

"Like a pig's arse, it is!"

"Shhh, Rolf. Don't upset her."

"Is he mad? Did I burn the toast again?" Yvette's voice was barely audible above the hissing of oxygen from the clear plastic mask covering her mouth and nose.

"I'm not sittin' around here. I'm going to find the guy who did this." Rolf squeezed Yvette's hand and left the first aid building. Didier took his place. He smoothed Yvette's sheet, took her pulse, wiped the hair from her eyes, all in one motion.

"Is she going to be okay?" Kerry could hardly get the words out.

"She has a guardian angel, this one. Some smoke inhalation, a bit of bruising, and a twisted ankle. I'm in touch with the emergency doctors at Dryden hospital and they want her kept here overnight. We can airlift her if we need to, if she gets worse."

"You know she'll only go with Matt."

"Then Matt it is." They sat quietly, watching Yvette's chest rise and fall.

"And how are you doing?" Didier asked.

"I think someone is trying to kill us." It was out before she had formulated the thought.

For once, he didn't laugh at her. "All sorts of near misses happen in the bush. You can't dwell on the 'what might have beens' or you'll drive yourself nuts. Do you want to stay here tonight? I can make up a cot for you."

Tears welled up in Kerry's eyes. The nicer Didier became, the worse she felt.

"You're okay; the shock is catching up with you. If you want a note so you can go home to your mom and dad, I can arrange it with Harcourt. I'll suggest you need stress relief, and it won't affect your employment record."

She didn't speak for a long time. "Thanks, Didier, but I could never leave Yvette. Especially now."

"Can I go back to our trailer?" Yvette croaked.

"No, we need to keep our eyes on you," Didier told her. "Actually, we should tie a rope around you."

"Very funny."

Kerry watched him calmly and efficiently ice Yvette's ankle and elevate it on a pillow. "How's that feel?"

"Fine, except now I'm freezing."

Kerry thought he was going to lean over and kiss Yvette's forehead, but instead he covered her up.

"It's none of my business, Yvette, but if you want to get out of here I can talk to Sirois and tell him you should be put on medical leave. He'd give you your walking papers, I'm sure of it."

"And miss all this excitement and overtime?" She coughed and tried to clear her throat. "No, no. I can't leave Kerry here on her own. Never going to happen."

"Maybe it's time you both left. Think about it, girls, because frankly, the fire boss isn't thrilled with either of you. You seem to attract trouble. Besides, it's an open secret that Kerry's afraid of the bush."

"She's learning. But okay, we'll think about it." Yvette yawned. "Did you drug me, Didier?"

"Hey, there are limits to my powers as a first-aider, super-qualified as I am." He put a finger to his lips and whispered, "Something from my personal stash, to make you sleep. Want some, Kerry?"

She shook her head.

"M-mmmmm, I like it." Yvette yawned again. "Kerry, are you there?"

Kerry reached over and took her hand. "Don't worry. I'm not going anywhere."

CHAPTER 19

The evening after the sauna fire, Kerry sat around the empty firepit with the rest of the kitchen help, waiting for Mr. Sirois to speak to the entire staff. She remembered another firepit, and a dance with Aubrey. What had possessed him to dance with her? Had he felt sorry for her because she was so quiet? Or because she was an outsider, like him?

"In deference to the *lady*, I'll clean up my language. Shut the hell up so we can get started," Harcourt said.

Kerry looked at the ground, silently cursing him for singling her out like that. She already felt small and lonely surrounded by three hundred men. Slash edged closer to her on the log they were sitting on as Harcourt introduced Mr. Sirois. "As if we don't already know who he is," he whispered.

"I need eyes and ears out there," the fire boss boomed. "Another hot spot started today in this quadrant." He whacked the flipchart with his pointer. "It's remote from the epicenter of the fire and the weather has been good, with no indication of lightning." He mopped his head with a handkerchief. "We've evacuated all the homes, trailers, and camps in this entire sector. There's no one left out there, as far as we know. So I'm asking you, because you've been out there—either flying or bulldozing or backburning. What's going on? Who could have set this new fire? We think it's the same guy."

Kerry closed her eyes, trying to be invisible. *Give me a break. Are they going to try to blame these new ones on Yvette?*

"Could it have been a campfire?" asked Didier. "Maybe somebody hiked in from outside?"

Sirois peered over his half-glasses at him. "Popular wisdom would say yes but I have my doubts."

"Any update on the pink lighter that was found on the island?" someone shouted.

"Nothing conclusive. Tiny little fingerprints that look like something a twelve-year-old boy might make," Sirois answered.

"I bet it was Two-Beers. He sure took off in a mighty hurry," someone else called. Kerry craned her neck around to see who had said that. *Aubrey was gone? When? How come she hadn't known?*

"What about the fire in the sauna? We heard something about a rock covering the chimney, forcing sparks back into the false ceiling. Is that true? Seems funny that Two-Beers has gone missing. What's he got to hide?"

"We're looking into that, okay?" Harcourt said. "It's being investigated by security, and if there's any wrong-doing, we'll deal with it. If anyone sees Aubrey Falls, send him directly to me, because I want to talk to that boy."

The men were fidgety and a murmur went through the group. Nobody believed this fire boss would do anything about the sauna fire, because it would be embarrassing for the department to admit on paper that it had nearly started its own wildfire. And as much as they taunted Aubrey, as much as they called him racist names, no one liked the idea that their own crew boss now seemed to be suspect number one.

"Aubrey!"

Kerry'd felt him brush up against her while she was washing coffee cups after the meeting, and she'd recognized his aftershave. She was so tired from doing all Yvette's work as well as her own that her reflexes were slow. When she turned her head to talk to him, he'd vanished out the side door, but not before slipping something into the back pocket of her shorts. Her gloved hands were deep in soapy, bleachy water so she couldn't immediately fish it out. Her mind raced, looking for an excuse to leave and read his note.

At about two a.m. Rolf called it a day. He was now bunking in the room next to the girls' and Matthew flanked the other side, all the better to guard them. Kerry reached for the flashlight behind the door and followed Rolf to the outhouse. She whipped the note out of her pocket.

"Meet me at the washing machines at 2:30 this morning." Aubrey had drawn a little arrowhead at the bottom of the page. She didn't have much time.

"Hurry up, Rolf, I'm tired."

She hustled Rolf up the hill to the trailer, threw on a long T-shirt as a nightie, and flopped on top of her bed. She waited until 2:25 to make sure Rolf was well asleep, then grabbed sweatpants and work boots and carried them outside. When she was fifty feet from the trailer, she put them on and started to run. Would he still be there?

"Aubrey?" she called softly.

"Over here."

She rounded the laundry building and there he was, a shadow in the doorway. He kicked the door closed behind her and led her to a bench in the pitch-dark. It wasn't until he kissed her that Kerry knew for sure. This wasn't Aubrey. Aubrey tasted of cigarettes.

Didier didn't.

"Let go of me!" she said, shoving him off the bench. "What do you think you're doing?"

"I wanted to see you." He switched on a flashlight and trained it on the ground at their feet.

"Well, you've seen me. I'm tired and I have to get up in two and a half hours."

"I need to talk to you about Aubrey. Kerry, there's weird stuff going on, and I need to know if it's true. I know you and Aubrey talk a lot so I thought maybe you could help me out."

"Why don't you ask him yourself?"

"Like everybody else, I can't find him. Do you know where he's gone? I really need to track him down."

Kerry wiped her mouth with the back of her hand. "And what the hell was that for?"

Didier shrugged. "You looked so cute with your hair all scruffy and your shirt shoved in your pants. I don't know; it was an impulse. I've been wanting to do that for a long time."

"Well, you can piss right off. You're not my type."

"And Aubrey is? You can do way better, Kerry."

"What the hell, aren't you supposed to be watching Yvette? You're not being very professional."

"You're right, I have to get back. But you'll let me know the minute he gets back?"

"Whatever."

When Kerry got off shift the next afternoon, she headed for the first aid building, where she found a pale Yvette sitting up in bed, hugging her body as if she were trying to keep it together. "Hey, you're looking good," Kerry lied. "I brought something to keep you company while you're in here." She pulled out her stuffed bear.

"Rover!" Yvette hugged him tight. "Thanks. I wasn't always like this, you know."

"Like what?"

"A wuss. Since Papa's accident, I'm not so aggressive when things are wrong. He'd be ashamed of me for not stinking up for that cat. 'Take a stand. Doesn't matter if you're wrong,' he'd say. 'You never go anywhere unless you have the courage to make mistakes.'"

"That would be 'sticking,' not 'stinking,' although some cats do stink. Quit being so serious!" *Pathetic. Yvette's shrinking into herself and I'm feeling farther away from Toronto every day that goes by.* "You'll be back to your old self in no time. I hate to say it, but it's too quiet in the trailer. I miss our little arguments. They let me know I'm alive. Oops, sorry."

"That's okay." Yvette smiled weakly. "I've been thinking that maybe I should tell them the lighter is mine and they could stop searching for me. What's the use? They're going to find out. Maybe it's better to tell them, and admit I don't know who's blaming me, and say I didn't do it."

"Oh, Yvette, you're just thinking about this because you're lying in bed with nothing to do. The consequences could be really bad, you said so yourself. I think we need to try harder to find out what's going on. What difference will a few more days make? Tell you what—while you're stuck in here, I'll step up the investigation."

"Maybe you're right. I won't tell them yet, but soon, because it's heavy in my mind." She sighed and shook herself as if she was mustering new courage, and raised her fists like a prize-fighter. "So forget about it for now. You want to go a round?"

Kerry answered by pouncing on her and tickling her, and finally letting Yvette win.

CHAPTER 20

L ater that same day, Kerry was folding tea towels in the laundry shed when Aubrey came up behind her, put his hand on the small of her back, and nuzzled her ear. She threw her arms around his neck.

"I should go away more often," he said.

Then she remembered and backed away. "Where've you been? They're looking for you."

Aubrey shrugged. "Who cares? The only thing that's important to me is the honor of my family. My mother deserves better."

"I don't understand."

He paused before he replied. "As you must know, I've never owned a shocking pink Bic lighter. I'm not a fire-bug. Kerry, you could help me clear my name."

Kerry was aware that, since Aubrey had become suspect number one, Yvette was less at risk. If she helped Aubrey, she hurt Yvette. But she didn't believe either of them had had anything to do with setting the fires. Maybe a better way of looking at it was that find-ing the real arsonist would help both of them. "I'm not promising anything, but what do you want me to do?" she asked.

"Just watch and listen," he said. "I'll drop by from time to time and you can tell me what you've learned. But there's something else. You can't talk to Yvette about this. She has—well, a bad attitude."

"How can I keep secrets from her? We're alone together for days and weeks at a time."

"You're more resourceful than you know." Aubrey touched her lips with his thumb, closing off her words and her breath. A long time passed, during which Kerry's mind raced and her knees felt weak.

"Okay," she said. "I feel like a total bitch but okay. I won't tell her I saw you and I'll keep my eyes open. I'll try. That's all I'm promising."

Aubrey smiled, an eyes, teeth, and ear-wriggling smile just for her. "Out of necessity, you'll learn how." Then he kissed the tip of her nose.

"Didier wanted me to tell you he's looking for you."

He slid his mouth along her cheekbone and brushed her lips like moth wings. He covered up her eyes. "You didn't see me."

She turned her head away. "I don't want to lie."

"Come on, Kerry, follow your instincts. Let your mind and heart work like friends—who love and trust each other." He chucked her under the chin but stopped short of kissing her again. "Trust yourself, Kerry. Take a risk. Tell him I was never here."

"Yvette, you're home! Whoa there, girl, what gives with the smoking? I thought we had a deal."

Yvette took a long drag and blew six linked rings toward the ceiling of the trailer. "Well, that's a nice homecoming. I'm just blowing smoke signals. Where've you been, doing heat leaps?"

Kerry snorted. "Don't patronize me. To think I actually missed you and I was looking forward to you coming home."

"Am I irritating you? It's usually the other way around." Yvette threw a dirty sock at Kerry's head.

"What's eating you?"

Yvette rolled on her back. "I don't like it when you go off on your own and I don't know where you are. It scares me. I get to thinking you aren't coming back."

Well, there's a switch. Kerry sat down on the edge of Yvette's bed. "I'm not going anywhere. Two by two, remember?"

Yvette sniffed the air. "Hmm, musk. So is there something you want to tell me? Where's your boyfriend these days? I heard he took off and they're looking for him."

"They're looking for you too—the one with the lighter, remember?"

"Piss off."

"Piss off yourself."

"I don't like him. Anyway, did I miss anything while I was away?"

"Are you kidding? Only the bears dancing on the roof of the cookhouse, trying to get in through the window screens. Didn't you hear Sirois shooting at them in the middle of the night?" Kerry said. "We've got to figure out what's going on here. You didn't steal a truckload of meat or start a fire and neither did Aubrey. Borrowing your necklace doesn't make him a thief . . ."

It was too late to take it back.

"Aubrey took my arrowhead necklace? You've known all along and you never told me?"

"Uhh . . ."

"You know how important that necklace is to me."

Kerry wished Yvette would fly off hysterically and just hit her. A rational, reasonable Yvette was harder to take.

"Where's he now?"

"I wish I knew," said Kerry. "I'm sorry."

"Do you see where playing social worker got you?"

"Yvette, he's not like what you think. He's well educated. He even speaks Spanish."

"Come on, what do you really know about him?"

"Enough. I think I love him."

"Get real. Maybe it's time I asked for a transfer, or just quit."

"I hope you won't." Kerry got up and stood looking out the window. "He asked me not to tell you stuff because you wouldn't understand. I didn't want to deceive you but it seemed easier."

"For whom?"

"What would have changed if I'd told you about the necklace, now that Aubrey is gone? I'd hoped to get the thing back from him and make it right. I can still try."

Yvette pulled a hoodie over her head. "Don't wait up."

"Where are you going?"

"To talk to Sirois about your boyfriend, the Indian thief." Yvette slammed the door behind her so hard that the trailer rocked on its foundation.

Kerry sat stunned. She had to find Aubrey to warn him. *Fast.*

CHAPTER 21

Next morning, after the breakfast rush, Kerry turned into a garbage vigilante as a useful way to deal with her anger at Yvette, and at herself for opening her big mouth.

"Save your energy, those bears will be back," said Slash, which gave Kerry an idea about how she could get to town. She said she needed specialized locks for the bins and asked Harcourt for permission to go. "The ones we got aren't working."

"Do you think we're the damn SPCA? Forget it, there's real work for you to do."

Kerry kicked herself for not going to Rolf first. Of course, when she asked him instead he said yes, and even made a crack about her being a substitute bear whisperer. She asked him for a grocery list, in case she was challenged about why she needed to go to town. *What am I doing? If Harcourt finds out, he'll fire me. But no, Rolf will stand up for me.* Once in town, armed with a grocery bag for cover, she looked everywhere for Aubrey and eventually came to the hotel tavern. He wasn't much of a drinker but it was worth a try. She walked up to the front desk, where a guy in a stained, sleeveless under-shirt was reading a dog-eared *Penthouse*.

"Yeah?"

Without luggage, she didn't seem like someone who needed a room. "I'm looking for my boyfriend . . ."

"Bar's right through there."

Kerry peered through a porthole window but strobe lights flashed like sheet lightning, and she couldn't see anything or anybody. Going in seemed like a bad idea. But what else could she do? She pushed open the door. Before her eyes adjusted, someone grabbed her arm and hustled her across the room, past the telephone boxes, the coatrack, and the pool table, into the shadows. He plunked her down hard on a chair.

"Look what I caught." It was Slash. He planted a juicy, sour tobacco kiss on her forehead. "Your bodyguard is the luckiest guy in here today."

Kerry shrank back in her chair as the server smashed a heavy tray of draft beer down in front of them. Slash lined up five glasses in front of her. "That's good for starters."

Kerry spotted the exit and was halfway out of her seat when Slash caught her wrist. "Drink up."

She picked up one sweaty glass and sipped at the head.

"Come on, down the hatch. Don't make me drink alone. I want to hear the story of your life."

Kerry threw the beer back in her throat and started to cough. He leaped up, lifted her arm, and patted her back.

"You all right? More for me, I can see. Waiter, we need some water."

Over the next ten minutes, Slash knocked back four glasses. "You're not much of a party girl, and I can tell this place is creeping you out. Let's go. I'll walk you back to the office."

He insisted. He even walked on the highway side of the road, with Kerry on the shoulder. They stopped dead at the entrance to the forestry office, where "Cops Are Pricks. Help Ursus Americanus. Home on Native Land" was spray-painted in fluorescent pink above the door. "Your boyfriend's getting reckless, taunting the cops to come after him."

"How can you be so sure it's Aubrey?"

"Who else knows the Latin for 'black bear'? For whatever reason, he's the angriest Metis I know. If I were you, I'd forget about Aubrey Two-Beers. He's a waste of space."

Kerry made a fist and tried smudging out the word "Cops." Aubrey was in real trouble, and she needed to find him before they did.

In the middle of the night, Kerry woke to the roll of a boat climbing up waves and falling down the other side. She didn't feel drunk despite the beer Slash had forced on her. She turned on her flashlight to see if Yvette was awake. It was three a.m. and Yvette's bed hadn't been slept in! She sat up, panicked about Yvette's where-abouts, until she remembered they'd had a fight.

She flopped down and the rocking of the trailer sped up. She heard a giggle, a man's deeper laugh, more rock-ing, a sound like beer cans opening, then more giggling. Boots clumping on the floor and heels, or maybe it was knees, banging against the thin, fake-wood paneled walls. Squealing in French, and much shushing.

They weren't in Matthew's room but one over. Kerry wrapped her head in a pillow and pretended hard that she was on a Caribbean cruise, and that the up-and-down of ocean waves was lulling her to sleep.

CHAPTER 22

The men came into the mess hall, inhaled their dinner, and left, continuing a day exactly like the day before. Conversation amounted to no more than "Pass the ketchup."

Kerry and Yvette were up to their shoulders in dirty pots. "Whoever's setting fires, I wish they'd stop," said Yvette.

Kerry was surprised that Yvette was talking to her again and was eager to prolong the conversation. "Must be a sicko," she said. "What's Matt's theory?"

"We try not to talk about work."

"Come on, you can wangle it out of him." Kerry could tell she was thinking about it.

Slash invited the girls for just one beer in his trailer when they went on break, mid-afternoon. *Why not?* thought Kerry. *If you can get over the look of him, he's a decent guy. Besides, he's obsessed with Aubrey and he knows something he's not telling. I can feel it.*

"Sounds good." Kerry didn't expect Yvette to come along but she did. After a couple of chugging contests between Slash and Yvette, which Yvette won, Slash had a brilliant idea for another game.

"You'll love it. It's a game of chicken. You run around in the dark in the dump and the first one to turn on his headlamp is chicken. Dead simple."

Kerry could feel her legs twitching with anxiety but she tried to keep her voice calm. "Sounds dumb. What's the point?"

"It's an initiation thing."

Kerry looked at her partner for help. "It's called Truth or Bear," said Yvette. "It's no big deal. I've played before."

Kerry's heart was stuck in her throat, and her voice squeaked as if she were sucking on a helium balloon. "How do bears come into it?"

Slash laughed. "You *only play* if there's a bear."

"And you walk around, and the first one to wimp out and turn on his headlamp loses," said Yvette.

"That would be me, within ten seconds."

"If you lose, you have to spill your guts about something dark and intensely personal," said Slash. "It's a great game. Don't worry. It's great; I'll protect you."

"Where's the dump?" Kerry asked.

"Just north of here," Slash said.

She felt panic flopping in her stomach like a caught fish. *Breathe in the nose and out the nose. Calm down.* Her mind raced. How could she turn this to her advantage? She had an idea, but could she bring herself to make Yvette choose between being a chicken and doing the thing she feared most? *You can do this, girl.*

"I know another dump," she said, and she reached into her shirt pocket, noting that her hands weren't even shaking. She unfolded the map she'd sticky-fingered from the office. It made sense that Aubrey was hiding out at the fishing cabin he'd mentioned. "This one."

"How do we get there?" Yvette asked.

Kerry turned to Slash. "I've been checking around about you." He took the match he'd been sucking out of his mouth, but his eyes never left her face. "You have a pilot's license but you don't fly. Why?"

Yvette sat up straight. "He does? I didn't know that."

Slash shrugged. "Busted! I *can* fly, but I'm taking a break. How'd you know? Have you been checking me out?"

Yvette looked uncertain. "How many years have you been flying?"

"I started when I was twelve, soloed at fourteen. I'm twenty-two now. You do the math."

Yvette let out a long breath. "This dump, it could be promising, but I don't like flying. Can I trust you?"

"It's up to you."

"Normally I only go with Matt but he's in Kenora and, like, you did save my life. See, there's this guy who broke into my trailer and stole something from me. Something that was my dad's. I overheard him talking about his fishing spot with Rolf. *It's* near a dump."

Slash raised an eyebrow. "Are we talking about Aubrey Two-Beers?"

"Yes! Since he stole Papa's good luck charm, I've had horrible luck!"

"Slash, we could do both things," Kerry said. "We could look for Aubrey on our way to play Truth or Bear."

He tapped the map. "This dump is in Sector 14. I could lose my job."

"Are you chicken, Slash? You chicken too, Yvette?" Yvette bit her lip. "Come on! Do you want that necklace back or not?"

"Quit pushing me! I don't know what to do! If Matt was here, I'd go."

"Slash will do fine. Make a decision, Yvette. He can't wait all day."

"It's a twenty-minute flight. If we leave before seven there'll be almost four more hours of light." Slash snapped the match in two and tucked it into the breast pocket of his shirt. "The fire boss is a New Brunswick boy, as am I, and I already put my application in to him to fly. He told me to keep my flying hours up in case they need me. I think I can sneak you on."

Yvette scrunched her face and held her nose as if she were jumping into the deep end of the pool. "Okay, okay," she said. "Let's do it!"

PART 4

Truth or Bear

July 10–15

As the helicopter lifted off the pavement, Kerry peered through the plexiglass floor at the swaying, blurring grass. Straight up and they hovered, then *zing*, like a dragonfly, darted away from the camp.

"I love this!" she said into her microphone. Slash gave her the thumbs-up.

Buffeted by every gust of wind, she felt cocooned in a bubble of motion. She turned around to see how Yvette was doing. *Poor thing has guts.* Yvette's eyes were closed as she chomped on gum and tried to block out the flight noise with her music.

It was fluky how things had fallen into place. Only twenty men had shown up for supper, because the fire crews had been ordered to camp closer to the fire as a fuel-saving measure. Rolf was happy to give his girls the evening off "to go to town," as long as they were back in time for breakfast prep.

The lies and deceptions prickled at Kerry but she swatted them from her mind. Her job was to find Aubrey and save him. He loved this land too much to destroy it by setting fires. She pressed her nose against the window, searching the banks of the lake below. *Aubrey, where are you? I'm so scared for you.*

Slash touched her arm, pointing out a bull moose grazing in a swamp, his rack of antlers huge and dripping with water. The moose started to run through the shallows head up, braying at the intrusion from above. Slash changed course, giving him a wide berth. There was no reason to stress the animal.

Miles to the left was the fire, a red festering sore, consuming everything in its path and spewing ash and smoke into the air. Kerry wrenched her eyes back to the burnover below. It looked like patches of black mold until she peered closer at the stripped skeletons of trees still standing, defying gravity. The fire was as vast and powerful as a tsunami rolling over the landscape, twisting and eddying and turning back on itself, leaving charred devastation in its wake amongst isolated stands of trees.

Slash touched Kerry's arm again and motioned to a burned-out cabin. There was nothing left but lumps of metal—a refrigerator, a stove, the remains of a water heater and an old truck.

"Crazy. Did they get out?"

He nodded.

Five more minutes and they were following a wide frothing river the color of maple syrup. Kerry didn't need to be told they were crossing into Sector 14; she'd memorized the map. She strained forward, looking for a dump, a waterfall, and Aubrey's fishing camp. A lake not far from the river, he'd said. Nothing. Nothing. *We'll never find it—omigod, is that it?* She felt like bouncing up and down on her seat but calmly directed Slash farther north.

Over the dump site he circled, looking for a place to land. He headed for a flat beach several hundred yards away, on the edge of a lake. The helicopter danced in the air as one skid lowered and then the other, until it kissed the ground. But as Slash was powering down the rotors the headset squawked, and Kerry was cut off from his conversation. He looked worried, now angry, now calm, like someone taking orders. "Copy that." He turned to Kerry. "A firefighter has a ruptured appendix and I have to go pick him up."

"Come on, really? This is the place, I can feel it," she said. "How long until you get back here?"

"Oh no, I'm taking you with me."

"We're supposed to be in town, remember?" Yvette piped up.

"I remember." He bit his lip. "Okay. Grab that pack there. It has a couple of sleeping bags, energy bars, and some flares. I'll be back before you know it. Don't start the game without me!"

No chance of that! They bent double and scrambled out, ducking low under the rotor blades.

"Wait, Slash, I changed my mind." Yvette waved at him to come back, but he misunderstood and waved as the helicopter jumped off the ground and buzzed off. *"Maudite marde!"*

Kerry watched the helicopter silhouetted against the sun until it darted into a cloud. Long after he was out of earshot, she convinced herself that she could still hear the thrum of the engine.

Slash is the only one who knows where we are!

She took the lead as they walked the path from the beach to the dump. She tried to imagine it in the dark, full of bears, with a scary game of chicken underway. *Not happening.*

"I don't think Aubrey would camp here," Yvette said. "We're looking for a well-hidden cabin."

They returned to the beach, selected another path, and had walked for about half a mile when Kerry heard voices. *Aubrey?* She backtracked and took a cut to the left. She was about to call out when Yvette yanked her to the ground, putting a finger to her lips. They wiggled commando-style behind a fallen log and watched. There was a perfect sight line from a forty-five-gallon drum in the middle of the clearing to a hunting blind high in a tree, and a hunter in green camouflage, sipping whiskey for courage.

A mother bear lumbered into the clearing and reached deep into the drum, scooping up a putrid chicken carcass. It took a bite and tossed the rest toward two cubs gamboling at the forest's edge, all the while sniffing the air.

BOOM.

He shot the mother in the head. Splinters of bone javelined across the clearing as the bear staggered and hit the ground, legs outstretched. Did Kerry only imagine the whimpering and squealing of orphaned babies scrabbling at their mother's teat? One of the cubs bolted and scratched up a tree, climbing higher and higher until it was level with the blind. The skinny tree whipsawed back and forth under the baby's weight.

BOOM.

The cub tumbled to the ground, a trickle of blood seeping from its mouth.

It was too much for Kerry. Her overstimulated brain withdrew from the carnage and focused instead on the surrounding details. Pink campfire smoke hung like gauzy curtains in front of a wall of jack pines. Whiskey jacks squabbled from tree limb to tree limb. Horseflies and dragonflies hovered—until another man dressed in camouflage squirmed in on his belly, elbowing closer to the drum where the mother bear and babies had so recently shared a meal. His bullet caught the other cub in the shoulder and it crawled, bawling, to its mother's side. With the next shot, it crumpled there.

Kerry felt sick to her stomach as she looked at the mother bear, its thick, glossy fur matted with blood. *How could anybody kill something that looks so human?* Death could not erase the obvious curiosity and intelligence on its face, as if, at the moment of death, it had been asked a puzzling question. She hugged her knees to her chest, unable to watch while the men dragged the bear away.

"This hunting is so illegal, and those guys are deaf drunk," Yvette whispered.

"Where'd they go?"

"I don't know. We need to stay here like little mice until it's dark and then go back to the beach."

"But they must have seen the helicopter drop us here?" Kerry asked.

"Doesn't look like it. They couldn't give a care."

"What about Slash?"

"We'll listen for him and run like hell when he comes. Stop talking."

For what seemed like an hour, Kerry lay facedown in the earth, her hoodie pulled tight with only her nostrils and mouth free. The mosquitoes whined in her ears until she thought she'd go mental. Keeping still was just about the hardest thing she'd ever done. Finally she couldn't stand it anymore, and she loosened her hood so she could see.

Soft, billowing green light, like shimmering veils strung on a clothesline, shape-shifted across the sky. Sparkles of starlight poked through like pinpricks. "Omigod, is that the northern lights?" she whispered.

"I like to say it's Papa, reminding me he's all around," said Yvette, stretching. "I'm a stiff and sore little mouse." She hauled Kerry to her feet and they started back the way they'd come, feeling their way in the dark with the help of the aurora borealis.

"I can't figure out why Slash hasn't come back," whispered Kerry.

"He's probably waiting for dawn. Me, I'm gonna kill him."

They bumped along, shoulder to shoulder, until they reached a clearing. That was when a rope slid over their heads like a lasso, snapping tight around them and jamming them together.

"I knew youse'd come out sooner or later," a man behind them sneered. "I be a patient man."

CHAPTER 24

"Who are you?" gasped Yvette. "Where are you taking us?"

"Shaddup!" The man pushed her from behind, whipping her head back and forth. "You don't know me."

He shone the flashlight ahead and shoved them along an overgrown path. Spindly trees were snapped and bent, as if something heavy had been dragged over them. When the girls struggled against the rope, he yanked it, slamming their shoulders against each other.

"Go right, and keep your yaps shut." They came to a small cabin, and he kicked open the door and pushed them through the doorway.

It was cool inside, but the air was so rank that it caught Kerry in the throat and she coughed uncontrollably. He pumped a Coleman lamp and lit it, the mantle glowing brighter and brighter as he turned the screw. Only when he held the lamp high did Kerry see the bear carcasses strung from steel girders, dripping blood. She opened her mouth to scream, but shut it as blowflies dive-bombed her on their way to the light and their sizzling death.

"Move!" He shoved them through a door into another small room. It took a couple of minutes for Kerry's eyes to adjust to the lamplight. The guy wore a greasy Blue Jays cap pulled over his face, obscuring his features, all except a scraggly graying beard. She searched for some sign that this might be Aubrey's cabin. A case of whiskey was open on the floor and a row of ten shot glasses snaked across a round plywood table, each touching the next, and partially full. Kerry's knees felt weak and she leaned against Yvette for support. Rifles stood behind the door, no doubt loaded and ready for bear. Or inconvenient visitors.

The man tied Kerry's wrists behind her back with twine but otherwise left her alone. Yvette wasn't so lucky. He patted down her thighs, her bum, her whole body, in such a sleazy way that, if she'd been Yvette, she'd have wanted to take a bath. Yvette kicked at him as he tied her wrists but he just laughed wheezily. He took off the ropes that bound the two girls together and shoved them onto chairs, tying them down where they sat. He walked out the door, slamming it shut and leaving them alone.

A surge of adrenaline rushed through Kerry's body. *Get out of here.* She worked at the ropes on her wrists, twisting and picking until she was sure her skin was bleeding. Yvette was doing the same thing with the same lack of success. She started sobbing.

"Yvette, please. Don't give up. You can't give up."

Yvette struggled to control herself, and finally shuddered to a stop. "I don't know what I did to deserve this," she wailed.

"Stop thinking like that. Nobody deserves this." Kerry tugged again at the ropes on her wrist, but it was no use.

"They can't let us go, you know. Not when we've seen all this." Yvette was starting to cry again.

"*Stop it!* We'll get out of here—"

There was commotion in the outer chamber, talking, stamping of feet. Both girls tensed, waiting for more poachers to come in. Instead, when the kidnapper walked in, Didier was right behind him.

"Didier? *Mon dieu*, I'm so glad to see you." Tears of relief streamed down Yvette's cheeks. "Look what this crazy man did! My arms are dying! Hurry and get this stuff off me!"

Didier didn't answer. He wouldn't even make eye contact.

"Omigod, it's you, Didier," said Kerry quietly. "You're the guy who's been setting these fires."

"What are you saying?" said Yvette.

"I'm gonna be sick," said Kerry. "I . . . we trusted you." Her right leg vibrated uncontrollably but she couldn't reach around to stop it.

"Whatcha wanna do with them, Didier? They can't stay here."

"Don't worry. I'm on it," Didier assured him.

"You'd better let us go, you piece of shit," said Yvette.

Didier smacked her hard across the face. Her head spun and the gold hoop in her ear sliced open her earlobe so that blood dripped along her jawline. She sagged in her chair and it almost toppled over.

"Don't hurt her!" Kerry screamed. Yvette seemed to be unconscious.

"As for you, bunny . . ." Didier advanced toward Kerry, swinging a roll of duct tape. He ripped a six-inch piece off with his teeth.

"Didier, please. Come on. Don't!" Kerry cried. "I'll be quiet. I promise. I won't say anything. Please, Didier! You can trust me."

"Too funny. Who flew you in here?"

Kerry hesitated, trying to figure out if it was better to lie to him or not. "Okay, it was Slash. But then he got a call to pick up a sick firefighter and take him to the Dryden hospital. He should've been back by now."

"Thank you." Didier grabbed her hair, yanked her head back, and slapped the tape over her mouth. "I have to make a call."

Hot tears streamed down Kerry's cheeks and she was helpless to brush them away. *I can't believe it's Didier! He's a maniac! He's never going to let us go.* She strained to listen to him talking on his satellite phone but couldn't make out his words. The skin on her cheeks pinched and burned as she tried to twitch the tape from her mouth. When he came back, he untied her from the chair, lifted her by the arm, and marched her outside. "Aubrey's camp makes a nice little base for us behind the fire line. I knew he wouldn't be using it while he was fighting the fire."

Kerry wrenched away from him, but her arms were still tied, and she tripped and fell to the ground. She struggled to roll onto her back. There was a truck parked in front of the cabin, with "White's Meats of Winnipeg" printed on the side.

Didier yanked her back on her feet. "Clever, huh? We steal a refrigerated truck, mix the bear bits in with the other stuff, so it looks legit if there's an inspection, give it a quick paint job, and off it goes to Toronto. The Yanks are happy with their trophy kills, and shooting bear out of season adds to the rush." He hauled up the rear door of the truck. "Get in."

The stench of dead bear was overpowering.

"Step over Big Mama. There's plenty of space at the back."

You can't make me, Kerry said with her eyes.

Didier grinned. "Yeah, I can. You can drop the other one up against the cub," he told his partner, who hoisted Yvette over his shoulder and threw her into the truck.

"Your turn, missy. Stay still while I tie your hands again."

When Didier tried to help her up into the truck, she pulled away. The bear was so broad that she could only get in by stepping over its head. She crouched down and leaned against Yvette's limp body, burying her face in Yvette's hair to keep from gagging and to avoid looking at Didier. She wouldn't give him the satisfaction. It was a small, very small act of rebellion. *You can do this, girl.*

"Sweet dreams, bunny. Your nose is twitching." Metal screeching on metal, Didier pulled down the door. She heard fumbling and a loud snap, and a grunt of satisfaction.

Finally, a door that locked.

CHAPTER 25

Every part of Kerry's body ached, but the pain in her body didn't come close to the pain in her heart. *Didier, how could I have been so wrong about you? You were so gentle with Yvette when she got hurt.* Her empty stomach heaved as she tried to block out the stench of dead bear. She couldn't think of an uglier death—drowning in her own vomit, forced into her lungs by the duct tape stretched over her mouth.

Hours crawled by. Yvette mumbled from time to time but she was too out of it to talk sense. The hunters came back to the cabin. Kerry couldn't tell how many there were but they were furious about having to give up their hunt and break camp without notice, and they swore at Didier and his partner. Finally, car doors slammed and motors gunned and the Americans were gone.

Yvette stirred. "Do you think he went and left us here? If he left us here, then—" The back door of the truck squealed open, and Didier's headlamp blinded them as he leaped in. "Out you get." He hoofed the dead cub out of the way.

Back on the ground, Kerry's legs gave out and she leaned into Yvette for support. Didier removed the tape from her lips but the sting of it went on forever. He cut the ropes off Kerry's wrists, but not Yvette's. "You, mademoiselle, are unpredictable—I'm leaving you tied up. And don't look so superior. Your boyfriend Matt is flying a group of hunters to Kenora tomorrow. Nice little deal he has on the side."

"Matt's working for you?" said Yvette. "I don't believe it!"

Kerry could feel Yvette's body begin to shake. "He's just messing with you!" she told her.

"And you, dancing queen, I found your boyfriend's lighter in a drawer. Not as pretty as your pink one, Yvette, but it'll do the trick. Catch, Kerry." He tossed it to her and she caught it. "Now, flick it open and set fire to the kitchen curtains. Don't look at me that way, just do it." She fingered the smooth metal of the old butane lighter, tracing Aubrey's initials etched in stainless steel.

"Those idiots in forensics will think Aubrey burned down his own cabin."

Kerry flicked the cap open and inhaled the fumes, stressing about what to do. She couldn't fight or run away with Yvette still tied up. Should she pretend to—

"Do it!"

Her hands shook so badly that she had a hard time getting the lighter to spark. On her fifth try it caught—but now what?

"Good. Set fire to the curtains and toss the lighter inside."

The lighter went out. Didier snatched it from her, lit it again, and held it to the dry old fabric. The flames climbed up the curtains to the moss chinking that sealed the space between the logs, and from there they traveled around the room.

"There's propane in there, let's go before it blows up!" Yvette tried to run toward the cab of the truck but Didier grabbed her.

"You're staying right here."

"Didier, we need to tie them up more," said the partner. "They'll get away."

"No, we're good. They can't walk out of here. When the bush goes up they'll fry, and the ropes will burn up. There won't be any evidence that something went down here. And in two hours we'll be in the States, chilling with a cold brew."

"What about the Sea-Doo?"

"Aubrey works for the department; he could have stolen it. A Metis who took off—how suspicious is that? That's probably as far as they'll look."

The flames were licking out the cabin window, climbing onto the roof and from there to the lower limbs of a feathery white pine. Yvette kicked and struggled in Didier's arms but he was laughing at her. "Look, honey, there she goes!" *Swoosh*—a wall of heat struck them as the flames leaped high in the air, and the noise of crackling and spitting wood took Kerry's breath away.

"Good luck, my darlings!" Didier flung Yvette far from the passenger door of the truck, into the bracken. In seconds the truck took off, but not before Kerry ran after them and grabbed onto the bumper. *Don't leave us here! I won't let you!* For about thirty yards she stumbled along, clinging to the truck, but as it picked up speed she couldn't stand the way her arms were being ripped out of their sockets. She dropped and rolled.

Yvette stumbled to her side and nudged her gently. "Kerry, are you all right?"

Kerry moaned and rolled onto her back, coughing. "Now-ow what?"

"I'm thinking. *Mon dieu*, think. There's so many roads back here, we'd get lost for sure if we try to follow the truck. Going to the left is not possible, as fire travels uphill faster."

Embers and flaming tree limbs were dropping around them, barely missing them. "Oh God!" Kerry grabbed Yvette and fumbled with the ropes on her wrists, finally freeing her. She made the decision for them both, and tugged Yvette into the bush on the windward side of the cabin, toward the lake. *Swoosh*— the forest was bright around them. *Why can I see where I'm going?* She looked up to see a crown fire racing through the treetops above them. *Run!*

CRA-A-C-K. CRA-A-C-K.

"Oh my God, who's shooting?" she yelled.

"Exploding tree," Yvette shrieked. "Run faster!"

At the base of every tree there was a trickle of flame, with smoke wafting skyward. "Yvette! Your hair's on fire!" Kerry swatted a red ember from Yvette's head without breaking stride.

When the propane tank in the cabin blew up, they were thrown to the ground behind a rock cliff, protected from flying debris. The heat and smoke were so intense that Yvette shoved Kerry's face in the moss, where there was still oxygen, until she could catch her breath. They scrambled downhill, crouching low, protecting their faces from whipping branches. *Too smoky to see. Where's Yvette? There!* Yvette darted ahead, then behind, then vanished in the smoke, then reappeared like a ghost. *I can't breathe. I have to slow down—no, go faster!*

Fifty feet to Kerry's right a tree torched, roaring like a jet engine and sending a scorching wave of heat in her direction. She covered her face with her arm and hurtled down a slope, banging her knee on a stump. She fell, recovered, then banged into another stump, sprawling flat. She spit dirt from her mouth and tasted blood. *Doesn't matter. Get up. Okay, crawl. Faster! You can do this, girl!*

"Watch out for the beaver stumps," Yvette shouted.

Now you tell me. Kerry breasted a wall of alders and thorny bushes ripping at bare skin, and hurled herself into the lake. The cold, silky water felt amazing on her stinging skin. She dunked her head, scrubbing the dirt and ash and stench off her body. The cold water shocked her back into action.

"Come on!" She swam and scrabbled over rocks along the shore, making her way to a spot on the water below the cabin. "I'm looking for—"

She didn't finish. Crashing into the stolen Sea-Doo the men had left behind, tucked under some cedars, she sloshed her way to the front of the machine and flipped open the dashboard. "Where're the keys? Yvette, look!" She dangled a set of keys for Yvette to see.

"Can you drive it?" Yvette could barely pant the words out.

"Maybe. We rented one in Florida. There's only one life jacket. You put it on."

The motor throbbed to life. Yvette jumped on behind Kerry and gripped her waist. Kerry let it rip and they raced into the middle of the lake, where she came to a stop. They watched the fire advance to the shoreline, inky smoke spiraling out of sight into the blackness, sparks spraying into the air like fireworks.

"Yvette, are you okay?"

"I've got something in my eye. It feels like glass. I'm pulling on my eyelid but it's not washing out. Auggh, check to see if there's a radio." She rested her head on Kerry's back while Kerry searched.

"There's this old thing. Hey, and there's a safety kit, with a flashlight." She turned it on. "And it works!"

"Okay, good," said Yvette, "but turn it off for now. Don't waste the batteries." She took the radio from Kerry and switched it on. "Pretty fuzzy. I don't think this is working. What time is it?"

Kerry peered at her watch. "Just after two."

"Mayday. Mayday. Can anyone hear me? Kerry Williams and Yvette Bernier here. We're on Barren Lake and there's a big forest fire. Mayday! Mayday!"

"It looks like we have half a tank of gas. I'm going down to the far end of the lake, away from the fire."

"Good idea, stick to the middle. And turn off the flashlight!"

Kerry strained to see in the dark as they moved steadily down the lake, the bow breasting a fine film of ash on the surface. On the shoreline to her right, straggles of smoke wended their way upward. Behind them, the bright orange glow of the fire was terrifyingly beautiful and surreal against a black velvet sky.

Kerry found it hard to move with Yvette's cold, damp body clamped against her back. Every minute or so, Yvette shouted into the radio. *Hopeless!* thought Kerry. "Quit squeezing me to death!" she said.

"Cut the motor. I saw something. There, flashing in that bay! It could be the hunters. Or Didier. In the dark we take the upper hand on them. He won't expect to see us. Listen how the sound travels over the water."

The men were arguing but their voices were unrecognizable. Then the lights of a plane blazed on and a motor throbbed.

"It's Didier, for sure," hissed Yvette. "Go back!"

Kerry turned on the motor and moved quietly around a point, to be hidden from view.

"It makes me sick that he'll escape. Me, I'd like to see him in jail for life," Yvette whispered.

"Is that Matt's plane?" Kerry said.

"I don't know. I hate them both."

Kerry dropped Yvette close to shore and tied the Sea-Doo to a tree. They scrambled across the point and watched the plane bobbing on the water. The longer she watched, the angrier Kerry became. *That bastard's going to get away,* she thought. *Yvette's right, he needs to be stopped.* She whispered a plan into Yvette's ear.

"You're nuts. But I think it would work if you did this." Yvette knew her way around the design of a float-plane and whispered back her suggestions. "The skirt of the Sea-Doo is maybe too low to make contact," she warned. "This maybe won't work."

Kerry got back onto the Sea-Doo. "Here, catch my fanny pack. Is your eye any better?"

Yvette shook her head and handed Kerry the life jacket. "Be careful."

From the shadows of a small bay, Kerry watched the men making their final preparations for takeoff. A guy on the pontoons leaped inside and slammed the door, and the engine accelerated. Kerry idled the Sea-Doo as the plane taxied out into the open lake. When it was even with her, she could see Didier in the passenger seat and his friend piloting. *Phew, not Matt. Yvette will be relieved.*

Kerry motored out about a hundred feet behind the aircraft, off the passenger side, staying well in the shadows as the plane taxied down the lake, turned back the way it had come, and got into position for takeoff. Its exterior lights—green, white, and red—flashed in time with her hammering heart.

Get mad, she told herself. *Think of those poor baby bears!* She let the engine rip. About fifteen feet from the left pontoon, she wrenched the handlebars hard to the left, smashing the side of her machine against the back of the pontoon. Remembering Yvette's warning, she took a second pass at the other pontoon and gave it a mighty kick with her work boots, a stomp worthy of any Riverdance champion.

She spun out in the dark and idled. *Did I do it? Was it enough?* She breathed in and out, trying to get her racing heart to slow down. The plane's motor whined low, as if it was going to stop, then revved again as the pilot tried to take off. The plane started to labor through the water. Kerry could see by the lights that it was off course, turning in a long, loopy circle. The plane stopped abruptly and tried again to take off, but again it plowed circles in the water. She held her breath. *We did it! Never in a million years would I have thought of smashing the water rudder. Thank you, thank you, Yvette, for being so smart!* Kerry yipped like a coyote and Yvette yipped right back. *This is the most amazing thing I've ever done.* Kerry gunned the motor and swerved crazily until she was around the point to safety. "Did you see that?"

"Shhhh, they'll hear you. *Magnifique.*" Yvette waded into the water to meet her and hugged her hard where they stood in the shallows, and when it was time to pull away she wouldn't let go. Kerry realized that Yvette was crying.

"I didn't know what to do if you didn't come back!" she said, through her tears.

"Shhh, you're okay. I'm okay." Kerry tied up the Sea-Doo and led Yvette to a spot on shore where they could watch as the men hung onto the struts and trained a powerful flashlight down onto the pontoons.

"You dumb asshole. You hit a freakin' deadhead!" they heard Didier say.

"It felt like somebody rammed us," argued the pilot.

Didier trained the flashlight along the shore and the girls dropped to the ground and held their breath. "Can you fix it?" he demanded.

The pilot didn't answer, but there was a weird swishing noise, and Kerry took a risk and looked up. "They're launching a rubber dinghy. We didn't think of that."

"Now for sure they're going to run away in the truck."

Kerry heard stuff being off-loaded into the dinghy, oars snapping into place, and then noisy, angry paddling. When the men passed by, she heard a slow exhalation and smelled tobacco smoke. She held her breath, certain that if Didier saw them he would use his rifle on them. She rolled over on her back, watching as his flashlight swept through the trees over their heads. *He knows someone's here. He'll never give up.*

Boom. Boom. Boom. Kerry covered her ears against the reverberations of a rifle echoing in the small bay. The truck door opened and slammed shut, the sound so clear that she felt as if she were right there beside them. She wanted them to hurry up and leave, yet she was livid that Didier was getting away.

"Choppers incoming," Yvette whispered. "They'd better hurry!"

Didier was having trouble starting the truck, grinding the starter motor as the key turned. He paused to fire three more rifle shots.

"Oh no," said Yvette. "Three of anything in the bush is an sos. He's sending out a signal. He's drawing the choppers to him!"

Kerry tugged her hand. "We'd be safer down the lake. I don't want them shooting at us." They scrambled onto the Sea-Doo and set out, barely moving across the water, flashlight off. When they were well out of rifle range, Kerry stopped and drifted and turned to look up the lake. "We're done for. Look at that!" An inferno of flames, shooting high in the air, was advancing down the shores of the lake, heading right for them. "There's nowhere we can go. The helicopters are our only chance. We have to get their attention."

"No! We don't know if the pilots are good guys or not. It could be Matt coming to pick up Didier. I think it was Matt trying to blame me for the fire and every-thing," Yvette said.

"Or it could be help answering your mayday call! Maybe somebody heard you."

"*Aucune chance.*"

Kerry's hand drifted to the switch on the flashlight. *Do I let her decide? Or do I overrule her? She's either paranoid or she's right. Which is it?* "We have to give up," she told Yvette. "It's our only way out."

"You can't quit! You're not a quitter!"

I'm not a quitter, but deciding to take myself out isn't the same as quitting. Kerry made her decision. The beam from the flashlight pulsed three times into the sky.

"I hate you! You're just like your mother!"

"You're nuts! Stop hitting me; this is our only chance!" She fended off Yvette's fists and continued to pulse the light off and on in sets of three. *s-o-s. Save Our Souls. Truth or Bear.* The first chopper changed direction toward her signal, coming closer. *Here they come!*

"We can hide from them!" insisted Yvette. "We can stay in the middle of the lake, away from the fire." But the smoke was already making them cough, and the fire was roaring closer.

The helicopter landed on the beach, spraying sand like shards of glass. Kerry closed her eyes and glided closer to shore, ignoring Yvette's tightening grip. *It's going to be all right. It has to be all right.*

The door slammed open. Matt was hunched in the doorframe.

CHAPTER 26

Yvette reached over Kerry's shoulder and gave the Sea-Doo some gas, trying to put it in reverse. *"Allez, allez!"*

Matt's face was lit by the landing lights from the helicopter, and Kerry couldn't keep her eyes off him. She noticed that he was wearing some kind of earpiece. Was he talking to someone? And what was that big bulge on his hip? *Is that a gun? Oh my God, Yvette's right! Matt is in this with Didier.* She tried to back the Sea-Doo away, pushing off from the bottom of the lake with her feet.

An arm swept Matt aside and Kerry was shocked to see Aubrey vault from the helicopter to the ground, shouting her name. *He's part of this too?*

"Wait, Kerry! You don't understand. We're here to get you out! We have to hurry."

"He's lying, Kerry," Yvette hissed. "He's up to his throat in this. We need to go quick, or they'll kill us."

But Kerry was thinking hard, wondering what to do. Surely Aubrey and Didier could never be partners. How could she be wrong about so many people? She turned the Sea-Doo toward shore.

"Mon dieu, t'es folle!" cried Yvette.

Aubrey sloshed into the water, grabbed Kerry off the Sea-Doo, and carried her toward the helicopter as if she were a small child. Matt was racing toward Yvette. Kerry heard the Sea-Doo's motor start up.

"No, Yvette, stop!" Matt shouted. His voice was drowned out by the whine of the Sea-Doo. Yvette swung it around and took off down the lake.

Yvette, come back! You can't escape the fire!

Aubrey bundled Kerry into the helicopter and belted her in as Matt was accelerating the rotors. As they took off, she looked down at the lake. Yvette was nowhere to be seen. She was gone.

Kerry awoke stiff and achy, compressed in clean sheets smelling of bleach. She squinted, taking in a pale green hospital room and an IV line snaking up from her arm. There was an oxygen tank beside the bed, but she wasn't hooked up to it.

Her memory was coming back. *Yvette! Omigod, where did she go?* She lifted herself up on an elbow and fell back with relief. Yvette was in the next bed, with one eye bandaged and her legs elevated. Her father's arrowhead was slung around her neck. *My brain feels as thick as smoke. What happened?*

"Knock-knock. Can I come in?" Buzz Harcourt stuck his head around the door. Kerry had never heard him ask permission to do anything. She didn't have the energy to tell him that she didn't feel up to talking to him. He came in and stood beside her bed. "You don't look so good."

"Neither do you, but thanks for making me feel better."

"I came to apologize," he said, pulling up a chair. "I should have protected you girls better. I am your supervisor, after all."

Kerry didn't respond right away. An apology was something, but could it make up for all the abuse he'd given them? "You didn't know we were going to sneak off with Slash—"

"Of course I did! That was part of the plan. I should have put my foot down and not let them talk me into putting you girls in the middle of this whole mess. It was supposed to be a harmless joyride for you, but then that guy's appendix burst and our plans fell apart."

"What are you talking about?"

"Slash is a cop—provincial police. Matt's a Mountie. That fake fire boss wouldn't know his ass from a fire hose—he's a cop too. They thought Aubrey was mixed up in the bear killings, and they figured you'd lead them to him. And then Aubrey would lead them to Didier and they'd wrap up the whole case. Sounded simple."

"Stop stop stop! Yvette has to hear this! Can you get her up?"

Harcourt took Yvette a glass of water and patted her hand, and she woke up. "Guess you didn't expect to see me so early in the morning," he said. She put a hand to her face and discovered the bandaged eye, but before she could freak out, he told her that she'd scratched her cornea and that was why it hurt so much. She was going to be just fine.

"Letting you girls out with Slash—well, I was against it but they talked me into it. Slash is a real pro and it all seemed innocent enough. I'm so sorry. It must have been hell. When you took off, Yvette, we didn't know what to do. Thank God that RCMP chopper found you."

"But how did you track us to the lake?" asked Yvette. "Did you hear my SOS?"

"We heard nothing on any radio, and we were monitoring all the channels. No, it turns out that Two-Beers is the real hero." Buzz picked up Kerry's fanny pack from the other chair. "Do you mind if I take a look?"

"Go ahead." Kerry got up on one arm to watch.

"Aha! Here it is. This little thing is a GPS tracker. It's normally used for following game. It seems Aubrey found a way to hide this in your bag without you knowing it. He was worried about your safety, but he didn't want to scare you. Then the damn thing didn't work— maybe you got it wet or it got wedged under something— but suddenly it came alive and Aubrey came tearing into headquarters to tell us where you were. I was out of my mind with worry. I was about ready to call your parents, and believe me, I wasn't looking forward to that."

He handed the disc to Kerry and she turned it over in her hand. She closed her eyes and held it to her chest. *So that was the real reason why Aubrey broke into our room.*

"My time's up. I'll drop by later and see how you're doing."

"Kerry, you okay?" Yvette said after he left.

"Fine, I think."

"I'm sorry I took off and left you. I really thought they wanted to kill us and you'd made the wrong choice about them. I was running on adrenaline, fearing about my safety."

"How about you? Are you okay?"

"Me? Sure! I have my lucky necklace back."

"Well, Mr. Undercover Mountie, how smart are you? You got your man but you nearly killed us in the process," Yvette said. "You used Kerry and me like bear bait to catch Didier in your stupid Sector 14." *They got him!* thought Kerry. *I never asked Harcourt about that!* "How many more cops were hiding at the camp, there?" added Yvette.

Kerry could tell that Matt was counting on his fingers. With every revelation Yvette squealed and repeated the name. Slash was the unlikeliest-looking cop, but in retrospect he was the most obvious. *Now I get it—he tried to get me drunk to find out what I knew about Aubrey's involvement.*

"I bet you thought I set the fire," Yvette teased.

"I'm not supposed to talk to you about any of this." When the girls started yelling at him, he held up his hand. "But I guess I can explain the parts that are public knowledge. It's all over the Internet, so there must be a leak somewhere. I figured the lighter was yours but you didn't have a motive. Didier has confessed to taking it from your back pocket, while you were dancing with him at the bunkhouse, and passing it to his buddy, who planted it on the island and set that fire to scare you girls away."

"Where's Slash now?" asked Yvette.

"Who knows? Assigned to another file. But I can tell you he was out of his skull with worry. See, we didn't know Didier's bear den was right there. We thought you were going to lead us to Aubrey's hunting camp, where Aubrey would be hiding. We figured that he knew more about what was going on than we did."

"And you were wrong and you nearly killed us!" Yvette said. "I hate you!"

"Hope not, because I just love you like crazy."

Yvette didn't answer for a while. "You're no Dudley Do-Right. You're married. Were you ever going to tell me?"

"How'd you guess?" Matt sounded surprised.

"There are some secrets, *chéri,* even the RCMP cannot know!"

"Yvette, I . . ." Matt shrugged. "We had a good time together."

"*Ç'est vrai*—take care of yourself, eh?"

"You stay safe," he answered.

"I will," she said, and after he left, "No thanks to you!"

Kerry heard grunting and puffing as Yvette struggled out of bed. "Men! I know you're awake; shove over." She lifted Kerry's sheets and wiggled in, resting her head on Kerry's shoulder. "I want my mother."

"Me too," Kerry said, and was surprised to realize that she meant it.

"Didier was such a beautiful boy. I don't know who to trust anymore!"

"You can trust me," said Kerry. She hugged Yvette until her arm fell asleep, along with the rest of her.

CHAPTER 27

L ike a water balloon pricked with a darning needle, the skies exploded with water, dousing the flames. The fire was over. They could go home! Rolf commandeered the cookhouse for an amazing send-off dinner. Special guests were invited, including the fake fire boss. Rolf said he might just pop him in the face, Mountie or no Mountie. Kerry thought she'd be right behind, if only for the sake of Mouser, who'd been kicked across the room "to help Sirois develop a relationship with Didier." It was Harcourt, ever the supervisor, who called the girls' homes and suggested that the parents talk to each other. Kerry's dad rented an suv big enough for Yvette's mother and siblings, their car seats, and all their gear. With three adults driving through the night, they would be here by noon the next day to take the girls home.

Yvette and Kerry volunteered to help Rolf in the kitchen. When he tried to refuse, Yvette insisted that she needed to keep busy to keep her mind off their ordeal. Both girls were running at half throttle, but chopping cabbage into coleslaw and slicing eggplant into moussaka took little energy.

"How'd it go today—the witness statement thing?" Rolf asked.

"Fine," said Yvette. "I don't want to talk about it." She slumped on the counter, resting her head on her arms.

"It sucked!" Kerry said. "The victim support lady was nice enough, and the cop tried to be nice when he asked me his questions, but he still videotaped me. I thought it would never end. I'm not even sure what I said. When it was over, I told him I had some questions but he said he couldn't answer them until after the trial—or the guilty plea, if we're lucky. And that might be two frickin' years from now! Would you believe I'm not supposed to talk to Yvette about the case? Or anyone else? We probably shouldn't be having this conversation right now. I'm *so* pissed."

"Pissed is healthy." He reached under the counter and brought out a bottle of red wine. He nudged Yvette. "Hey, you—you still on medication?"

"Only sleeping pills at night," Kerry answered for her. "We're good." She held out her glass. "I feel like Didier is still controlling us—manipulating us. I want to punch something!" Instead, she took a long slurp of wine and Rolf filled up her glass.

"Well, I didn't sign anything," he said. "It's front-page stuff, for God's sake. No harm in you listening to me read it out."

"Doubt it," said Yvette. She covered her ears.

"Go for it, Rolf. I want to know *everything*."

Rolf read snippets from the paper, editorializing as he went, sketching in the details, some of which they already knew. "Didier Hart of Dryden, Ontario, has been charged with arson, kidnapping, attempted murder, and various other offences, including poaching bears out of season and running an illegal hunting camp for several summers. He and his accomplices, who stretch as far as China, set fires to divert attention away from the bear killings. A joint operation of the RCMP and Ontario Provincial Police has been investigating the bear poaching since last summer but they made no connection with the setting of fires until this year, because of the dry weather. Bear parts were being smuggled internationally to Asia and cities along the U.S. Pacific coast."

Rolf looked up. "I left out the part about the kidnapping. You're named, Yvette, but Kerry, you're a minor so you aren't listed here. Some head of police investigations is calling you two 'resourceful' and 'courageous.'"

"Just covering his ass," said Kerry. "Is there anything in there about Sector 14? That's the part I don't get."

Rolf put the paper down. "Nope. This is what I've learned from my sources, who shall remain unnamed. The cops figured out approximately where the business was based, by assessing the ignition points of the fires, and that was why they imposed a no-fly zone in Sector 14—hoping that Didier's guys would relocate there and they could contain them. The arson was supposed to keep the cops away from the bear killings, but it actually ramped up their investigation. With the wildfire devastating so much forest, and closing down mining and lumber operations, the companies and the government piled on the pressure. They wanted it stopped—the fires, the smuggling, the whole stinking mess. And then they completely cocked it up by involving you two girls.

All I can say is, thank God for Aubrey or we wouldn't be having this conversation." He drained his glass to the bottom and poured himself another one. "I predict more charges, just wait and see."

"You can't just leave that hanging out there!" Kerry said. "What else aren't you telling us?"

"Let me ask you this. Does any good trucker bring back an empty load? Do you think Didier's the kind of guy who'd smuggle big screen TVs from Asia?"

"Drugs," Kerry breathed. Rolf made a motion to lock his lips and throw away the key.

"*Mon dieu*. Tranquil waters run deep," said Yvette.

They'd been so lucky. Kerry couldn't wait to finally see Aubrey and thank him in person. He was back on the fire line, but he'd sent cards and flowers while they were in hospital. She wondered how her mother was going to react—after all, Aubrey had saved her daughter's life!

Phew, it's hot. Kerry slipped outside for some air and watched her partner through the screen door of the cookhouse. Yvette's eyepatch was gone but she had to wear sunglasses, even indoors. *She looks like a drug dealer herself, topping and tailing those wax beans and shooting little yellow bits around the kitchen.* Kerry took the keys to the truck out of her pocket and dangled them so Yvette could see them through the window.

"Rolf, I'm going outside for a smoke," Yvette said, giving Kerry a "what's up?" look.

"Let's take a ride." Kerry tossed Yvette the keys and she tried to give them back. "Come on, Yvette, there's nothing wrong with you. We need a break."

Yvette gave in and took the wheel. She skirted the

town to avoid the transient workers drinking away their paychecks, finally turning off at the department offices by the lake. Kerry took her work boots off and walked the length of the dock in bare feet. She rolled up her pant legs and stepped down the ladder into the water, letting it lap around her knees. She surveyed the green shoreline, the sprinkling of islands, the eye-squinting dazzle of sun on water. "Amazing, isn't it?"

"Sun feels good. Aren't you afraid of getting a leech?"

It was good to hear Yvette laugh again. "After what we've been through," Kerry assured her, "a love bite from a bloodsucker isn't on my scale of things to worry about. Besides, you'd save me. Again."

Kerry let agonizing minutes go by before she managed to dish what she needed to say. "Yvette, I don't want to go home yet. I want to work for the rest of the summer but I don't have the guts to do it without you. Do you think you could blow your mom off and finish the time out with me?"

"Huh, you just want to stay near your boyfriend."

"That's only partly true. I really like him, but this fire has made me think about my life. I'm seriously thinking about quitting dance, but I need more time to decide."

"Are you nuts? What about all your friends?"

"What if I don't have what it takes? What if I can't have a professional career? Do I want it *enough?* Do I want to wreck my body down the road? Is a career in dance what I really want, or just what my mother wants? And what friends? I haven't heard from anybody. I want friends I can count on, not friends just because of what we do together."

"Like you and me. Fire buddies."

Kerry got out of the water and grabbed Yvette by the shoulders and shook her. "Fire buddies, my ass. Given what we've been through, we're stronger than blood brothers. Blood sisters!"

Yvette started to laugh. "Ooh, I think you're turning French."

"It could happen."

"Me, I can't stand to be in the same room with Aubrey. I can't forgive him for stealing my necklace, and I don't buy his excuses. He could have talked to me about how it hurt him that I had an artifact—as he called it—that belongs to native people."

"You're entitled to be mad at him. But come on, he wrote and apologized. I believe him when he says he took it impulsively, and then didn't know how to give it back. He still hopes you'll donate it to a museum or somewhere. For God's sake, Yvette, we owe him our lives."

"I'll give it away when I don't need it anymore."

"You never needed it, Yvette. Look what you did without it."

"And look at you. So skinny, but made of steel."

"Right. When my mother gets here, we'll know for sure if I'm any tougher. Honestly, I'm afraid that if I go home now, I'll get sucked back into my old routine. I need more time away from her so I don't cave just to get her off my back. I want to make up my own mind about my life. Please stay with me for the rest of the summer." She stared Yvette down, trying to get a yes out of her, but Yvette wouldn't meet her eyes.

"Remember how I said you were just like your mother?" Yvette said finally. "You used me. You wanted to find Aubrey and you worked it so that I would fly with Slash. You knew I was afraid, but you threw me into deep water anyway. We are lucky we came out of this alive."

Kerry was stunned. Was Yvette right? Was she starting to manipulate people like her mother did? It wasn't a pretty thought.

"I'm so sorry, Yvette. I can see how you might feel that I threw you under the bus. But I did it for the right reasons. I just—in my bones I knew that Aubrey hadn't done it. And I hated your attitude toward him. I thought solving this would help all of us. Can you forgive me?" She crossed her fingers and waited.

"It's true that I still need the money." Yvette looked across the water at the shoreline as if seeing it for the first time. "So, I don't like Aubrey very much but I accept that he showed guts and good sense. That's all I can say. At least until I get to know him better. Okay, maybe I could stay here for the summer—if you promise to do all the cooking and dishwashing. I never want to see the inside of a frying pan again!"

"Deal!" Kerry grabbed her and hugged her. "Oh, we're going to have fun!"

The girls linked arms and walked back to the truck. While Kerry hopped on one foot to put her boots back on, she spied their steel boat tugging on its line, anchored just off shore. "Look, that thing keeps following us. It's an omen."

Yvette backed the truck down to the launch ramp so they could hoist the boat into the back. "One, two, three!" they yelled, and the rust bucket seemed to fly into the back of the truck.

"It's lighter than I remember," Kerry said.

"You grew into it. Look at those muscles!"

Kerry faced the water, scanning the shoreline. The air was clean and pure after the rains, like spring water. The seduction of the bush tugged under her skin. It felt right—this wall of green trees, the blue skies, the constant gurgle of water lapping on granite.

Would she continue to dance? There was time to think about that. Thanks to Aubrey, she'd been given the gift of a summer in the bush to figure out her life. One thing she knew for sure—she didn't want to turn into her mother.

"Hey, my friend, I could do with some help here!"

Kerry had an overwhelming feeling of déjà vu, a flashback to their first day, when Yvette needed help with her gear. But *friend* was something new. She liked the ring of it.

Friends through fire.

Friends for life.

Anything could happen.